BOULDERS OVER THE BERMUDA TRIANGLE

Published in Canada by Engen Books, St. John's, NL.

ISBN-13: 978-1-989473-88-7

Distributed by:
Engen Books
www.engenbooks.com
submissions@engenbooks.com

First mass market paperback printing: October 2020

Cover Design: Ellen Curtis

Slipstreamers Committee:
Amanda Labonté
Ali House
AJ Ryan
Ellen Curtis
Erin Vance
Lauralana Dunne
Matthew LeDrew

BOULDERS OVER THE BERMUDA TRIANGLE

PETER J FOOTE & JD RYOT

CHAPTER ONE

"Rescue ship to Cassidy Cane, come in Cassidy," the voice crackled over the speaker that bounced like a Hawaiian doll on the dash of the experimental plane.

Jamming the steering yoke between her knees, Cassidy risked taking one hand off the vibrating yoke to flick the radio on.

"Cane here, kinda busy at the moment, you want something in particular?" Cassidy said as she tucked the loose strands of her hair behind her ear, before taking the yoke again.

The speaker crackled once again before emitting a blast of static that was strong enough to drown out the struggling engines of the aircraft. The static faded in intensity and Cassidy could make out the words coming from the ship far below.

"We're having a hard time keeping you in our sights, Cassidy. The storm is growing and the cloud cover is getting thicker. Please report your status."

"My status?" Cassidy muttered under her breath as she looked out the windscreen of the plane. Wipers beat a rapid tempo to push away the drawing rain, but did little except add to the overwhelming din within the cockpit. The altimeter read 27,000 feet and climbing, while the fuel gauge was at less than half and falling fast as the engines struggled against the storm. An instrument panel with more lights, readouts, and gauges than she knew what to do with or even what they did had Cassidy shaking her head.

"How did I let Gamgee talk me into this...?"

***

"Just think of the possibilities, Cassidy!" Dr. Gamgee exclaimed as he brandished his hands in the air and paced from one end of his cluttered lab to the other. Without knocking over any of the precariously placed pieces of equipment that threaten to avalanche at any second, he spoke again. "If we could make a practical radio that provides contact between dimensions, we could expand the frontiers of human knowledge to limits never dreamed of," Gamgee said as he removed a handkerchief from his vest pocket, using it to clean his glasses while staring along his nose.

Cassidy, perched on the bare corner of a cluttered table, stared back. Twisting her long braid between her fingers, Cassidy did her best not to disturb anything in the workshop. Health and Safety had never been a priority for Gamgee or his inventions. "So before you get yourself too sidetracked, let's start at the beginning. Rocks are dropping out of the sky...." she lead Gamgee.

"Ah yes, the meteors," Gamgee muttered, replacing his glasses. "The Bermuda Triangle has been the home of the strange and unbelievable since the Spanish first sailed that part of the Atlantic."

"Sorry to interrupt again, Doctor, but that's inaccurate. The 'myth' of the Bermuda Triangle is just that, a myth, perpetuated by authors to manufacture an enigma when logic will produce the answer." Cassidy proceeded when Gamgee beckoned her with his handkerchief. "It's basic environmental science. Any decent researcher will tell you that areas frequented by tropic cyclones and unseaworthy vessels have a high probability of disappearances."

His cheeks turning red, Gamgee gave a pointed nod and replied: "Perhaps you're right, but that doesn't explain this," he said, and with a melodramatic flourish, whipped off a sheet from a crowded table.

Her interest piqued, Cassidy wandered over to the table and peered at the lump of rock that had been underneath. Pulling a magnifying glass from her shoulder bag, Cassidy leaned in to examine the medicine ball-sized rock as Gamgee continued his account.

"Setting aside the history of the Bermuda Triangle, I can tell you some facts," Gamgee began, his tone taking on the smooth cadence of one used to speaking to crowds. "Meteors entering the earth's atmosphere aren't anything unusual; it happens countless times a day. Though few meteors are the size of this one. Until now no one has suggested that they entered from anyplace but our own solar system."

Cassidy's attention piqued, she interrupted her study of the meteor. "You're suggesting that this rock came from another dimension?"

"Yes, for three reasons," Gamgee said, and started ticking off his fingers. "One, there isn't any sign that this rock suffered atmospheric reentry, no melting or heat stress. Two, metallurgical analysis reveals this rock is unlike anything ever found on earth before, and three, a cruise ship sailing in the area witnessed the rock falling through a portal."

"You realize you could have lead with that," Cassidy muttered. "Okay, I believe you. It sounds probable this rock came from another dimension. How is it worthy of exploration? What makes this one so extraordinary that it jumps to the front of the line?"

"That's an excellent question, my young friend," Gamgee replied. "When the divers returned from the crash zone, they brought back several fragments, but this piece had something unique within it. A green crystal embedded into the rock, which displayed some fascinating properties." Gamgee was becoming excited, once again pulling out his handkerchief but this time using it to mop his brow, and allowing Cassidy to notice fresh scrapes on his arm. "I damaged the crystal in a lab accident and it splintered into two fragments. While investigating afterward, I discovered that some power still linked the pieces in a way I don't understand. I observed light and sound aimed at one segment manifest in the other, like a reflection."

Playing with her braid, Cassidy puzzled out this discovery. "That's delving into quantum mechanics, isn't it? Connections between things even when the cause isn't apparent?"

Gamgee's eyes widened, and he gave a reluctant nod.

"Hey, my focus might be archeology, but I'm well read," she replied.

"I'll remember that. As I was saying, these crystals have the potential to remain connected after we cleave them. I've postulated that we could create old-fashioned crystal radios that provide instantaneous communication between vast distances and even dimensions. But to have a working prototype I require more of the crystals to experiment with, and that's where you come in Ms. Cane."

CHAPTER TWO

"Repeat, Cassidy, we can hardly understand you."

Jarred from the memories of her briefing, Cassidy realized the storm that had been on the horizon now surrounded her. Remembering that the rescue ship was awaiting her response, she yelled over the buffeting wind, creaking plane, and crashing thunder.

"I said," Cassidy looked into the sky and watched the swirling portal in the storm's centre. "I said," she reiterated, "maybe Gamgee was correct about a portal in the skies above the Bermuda Triangle."

Both hands white-knuckled the plane's yoke, and Cassidy watched as the compass mounted to the dash of the plane spun one way then another, as if it were tipsy and staggering its way home from the bars.

"Great... what else could go wrong?" Cassidy muttered as she banked the plane against the hurricane-force winds. Perhaps in answer to her query, a bolt of lightning flashed, leaving spots in her eyes and half the plane's electronic panels dark, including the radio.

"Just wonderful... me and my fat mouth," Cassidy cursed as her brief glance out the window confirmed what she felt in her heart. Billowing clouds filled the sky, with no trace of the rescue boat nor the roaring waves of the Atlantic Ocean. The dying glow of the fuel gauge, that showed less than half full, highlighted her. "Nothing to do but get on with the mission then." The grin on her face might have been considered mad, considering her desperate circumstances.

Trusting that the plane's homing beacon was more heavily shielded than the other electronics on board, Cassidy slapped the huge red button and exhaled through clenched teeth as it pulsed a steady red, matched by the homing device on her wrist.

Leaning forward, Cassidy could pinpoint the portal now. She and Gamgee had speculated that the Bermuda Triangle portal would be parallel to the ocean, and it turned out they were correct. Cassidy doubted she'd ever know whether the storm or the portal were here first. What she realized was that the portal to the dimension where the crystals had originated was another 10,000 feet above her.

Once again, Cassidy used her knees to hold the bucking yoke to control the plane from becoming captured in a murderous crosswind and spinning out of control. Tightening her seatbelt until it dug deep, she tugged the harnesses on the parachute strapped to her back to reassure herself that it was there. Next she picked up the oxygen mask Gamgee had insisted that she pack and turned on the flow.

As prepared as she could be, Cassidy used her wiry arms to yank back on the steering yoke, forcing the nose of the experimental plane to point in the general direction of the portal. She engaged the booster rockets strapped to the frame of the airplane. The punch was immediate and unpleasant as it thrust Cassidy deep into her chair, her arms striving to keep the plane in line with her target.

"Why does this blasted thing have to be so tough to get to?" she yelled through gritted teeth.

Thirty seconds of acceleration later, loose articles in the plane bounced around like socks in the dryer. Cassidy watched as gauges spun, their numbers meaningless at this stage, and as the swirling portal loomed larger.

Every rivet on the airplane seemed to rattle loose, but Cassidy's face was alight with pleasure. A surge of adrenaline coursed through her veins and she screamed out in delight as the nose of the plane pierced the portal.

The howling storm over the Atlantic Ocean disappeared into silence, and Cassidy saw stars.

***

The void of the vacuum of outer space rushed into the cockpit of the airplane. The only thing that saved Cassidy from a sudden death was the oxygen mask over her face.

Sadly, it couldn't help her from the cold, which sought to strip her body of its warmth and vitality. In seconds the sensation was leaving the tips of her fingers and toes as she grappled to think and not allow panic to set it.

With the frosting of her face mask making vision difficult, Cassidy turned her head side to side to see the mess Gamgee had dumped her into this time. The faint flashing pulse of the red homing beacon on the dash and her wrist provided a slight comfort, though how that would help in outer space she didn't know. The remaining controls within the airplane were dead, only the emergency batteries were available, and Cassidy didn't know how long they would last in outer space.

Hitting the emergency clasp on her seatbelt released the pressure against her. Doing so disorientated her; the absence of gravity carried her forward until it forced her face up against the front cockpit window.

The black of the void was stifling. Emergency lights along the wings of the airplane did little to penetrate it, but shifting shadows resolved themselves into tumbling asteroids and it explained the question of the alien rocks.

"Just marvelous. Gamgee said nothing about outer space," Cassidy said. Ice crystals crackling on her face mask and her supply of oxygen hissing in her ears were the only noises she heard in the soundless void.

Cassidy struggled with frozen hands to unlock the canopy's release mechanism. On her third try, she got her fingers around the lever and tugged. Tiny explosions vibrated through the plane and it blew the canopy clear of the fuselage, leaving Cassidy exposed to the vacuum of space. Her breathing ragged, vision blurring, Cassidy struggled to think straight and not give in to the appealing call that she just close her eyes and go to sleep.

"Lights... I'm sure, light," she whispered, as her sluggish mind forced itself to accept what her eyes were showing. A broad grouping of lights twinkled and shone through the dancing asteroids. Spending the last of her waning strength, Cassidy Cane pushed away from the airplane, into the unknown.

CHAPTER THREE

"Now Agnoix, I want you to promise to listen to your brother. If he tells you not to enter a section of the station, you don't go in. I don't care what the other youngsters are doing, if they're seeking to get a glimpse at alien visitors, you are to remain within the Xik'en zone. Do you understand? And Axaik, I appreciate this is your last time to enjoy Sastreni before you enter the ranks of adulthood. I'm only letting you go if you agree to watch your sister and keep her safe," Orlol said from the kitchen as she used her prehensile tail to hold a giant mollusk. With long experience she extracted the struggling creature, plopping it into the steaming stew pot.

Axaik stuck his forked tongue out between needle-sharp teeth at his sister, but retracted it when Orlol walked into the living room, cleaning her hands on a cloth.

"I asked a question; did you hear me?" Orlol asked her offspring, her reptilian eyes narrowing until the two siblings settled and intoned "Yes, mother," in unison.

"Good. I realize you two have your father wrapped around your talons, but while he's outside the star system trading, and buying you," Orlol pointed a talon tipped finger at Axaik, "an apprenticeship with the trade guild, I'm in charge and I won't have my children being the gossip of this space station."

Orlol's posture relaxed as she made herself understood to her children. "Okay, let me have a look at your costumes. Agnoix, who are you supposed to be again?"

Straightening her homemade mask, Agnoix replied: "I'm Brauxel, the Warden of the Two Divines. The Saint who championed the destitute, as well as the rich and powerful. Our rulers executed her for non-traditional Xik'en beliefs."

"Ah yes, and your father approved this choice didn't he? I'm uncertain this is a true role-model for you. A proper Xik'en should lift themselves up, not rely on others," Orlol said, holding up her taloned hand in resignation as Agnoix opened her mouth to argue. "I appreciate you have different points of view and wish things were different, but this is reality. You'll be an adult soon, required to be a functional part of Xik'en society, not a careless dreamer like most of the aliens that frequent this mining station. Please, just think about who you wish to be for the rest of your life."

Turning her attention away from her daughter before they got into one of their frequent and repetitive arguments, Orlol addressed her oldest child. "And you're honoring Tox'eix once again, correct? The architect of the Xik'en Interstellar Empire?"

Rolling his shoulders in a gesture of bravado, Axaik flicked his tail and bowed to his mother. "Who better to celebrate tonight than the reptile who founded our Empire thousands of years ago?" He adjusted the sweeping white robes decorated with golden stars and talons, a handmade copy of the one worn by Tox'eix. Axaik curled his lip, exposing needle-sharp teeth at his sister when she turned to open the airlock of their residence.

With the airlock door open, Orlol bid her children farewell.

"Remain together. Honor our ancestors with your games and puzzles, eat nothing not given to you by fellow Xik'ens, and be home before the next shift change in the refinery. I'll have mollusk stew in the food saver for you. I'll be straight home after my shift in ore processing."

As her children fled the residence, Orlol allowed the airlock to seal, then hastened back to the kitchen where the mollusk was trying to escape her steaming pot.

"I swear, those kids will be the death of me," she complained.

***

"What are we doing here, Axaik? You promised Mom that you'd escort me through the residence sections to show off my costume for Sastreni and get candied treats."

"You don't want to do any of the stupid kid stuff do you? This is my last year to enjoy Sastreni and I will not waste it knocking on doors for a slice of fruit leather. Me and my friends will have a proper party, and if you want to fit in you'll come along," Axaik said as he watched to make certain they were alone before rapping a series of taps on the maintenance hatch. The hatch lock squeaked, swung open, and a gaggle of near adult Xik'ens tumbled out.

Even in their inaccurate costumes, Agnoix recognized them as her brother's classmates. Other Xik'ens on the verge of maturity, many of whom would waste their lives counting shipping crates or repairing mining pods and feeling they had life by the tail.

Skipping backward as the landslide of hyper Xik'en youth tried to wedge themselves back into the maintenance tunnel, Agnoix pleaded with her brother. "Come on, Axaik, you promised and I even said I'd give you my treats from Sastreni tonight. What will Mom say?"

Agnoix realized that she had crossed the line when her brother stomped up to her and gripped the front of her costume, his sharp talons ripping the cheap fabric.

"Now listen here, alien lover. If you don't want me to tell Mom how you're missing classes to slink into the forbidden mammal section, you'll say nothing about this," Axaik hissed, his hot breath right in her snout. "Do we understand each other?"

Agnoix could do nothing but nod, her mask slipping on her face. His point made, Axaik released his sister, tearing more of her costume.

Baring his pointed teeth, he swung back to his companions and said: "Get yourselves together. We have a party to make happen and we don't need any alien lover to hamper our style. Let's move!"

With a generous measure of pushing, the group of young Xik'ens charged down the narrow maintenance corridor packed with pipes, wires and metal catwalks. Axaik flicked his tongue along his razor-sharp teeth and closed the maintenance hatch with a loud bang, leaving Agnoix alone in the hallway.

CHAPTER FOUR

Abandoned by her brother, and stung by his words, Agnoix fled without heed to her destination. Tears streamed down her scaled face, making her vision issues worse as Agnoix raced through the halls, past others out enjoying Sastreni. There were squeals of laughter as parents with small Xik'en children and older kids garbed in colourful costumes offered deference to the role-models of Xik'en society with treats and games. Blinded by tears, Agnoix brushed past a small group only to stumble, then stop in a maze of limbs and tails.

Her mask slipped off and Agnoix found herself snout to snout with a crying child and an irate parent.

"I should have known. You're that Agnoix, aren't you? Orlol's daughter? Always making trouble, upsetting your poor mother, wait until I see her..."

Agnoix didn't listen to any more of the woman's ranting. With the angry parents' shouts ringing in her ears, she scooped her mask up off the floor and rushed away.

The energy provided by embarrassment and shame soon failed her. Agnoix collapsed against the cool glass of one of the mining station's many exterior windows. Heav-

ing lungs struggled to bring in fresh air and ease the sob-
bing that had overtaken her. After a pause, she regained
her composure and took in her surroundings.

Her mad rush through the halls of the sprawling mining station had brought Agnoix to a quiet, seldom-used
space. Unlike the grand viewing galleries, where the trade
ships, space yachts, and other vessels arrived and depart-
ed the space station, Agnoix was in a smaller gallery. Her
view showed where the mining pods and tractors towed
in the various ore rich stones from the asteroid belt into
the mining complex.

Standing, Agnoix looked past her reflection in the
thick glass. Past the shamble of the costume she'd spent
weeks bartering materials to produce, and stared into the
graveyard of rocks that brought her species here.

It was taught to every school-aged student that this
massive asteroid belt that the great Xik'en Empire laid
claim to centuries ago was within the Vao 63I system. The
asteroid belt was once two planets that collided millions
of years ago. There were other planets within the star system. The Xik'en ignored them because they were without
atmosphere or material significance. 'Vao' referred to the
asteroid belt and mining station within it.

Every minute of every day, mining pods piloted by
Xik'ens jetted through the crowded belt and assessed the
remnants of those two planets, tagging them based on
their mineral property. Then, depending on demand and
market conditions, her people carved up those asteroids
in space and hauled the chunks to the ore processing part
of the station. Agnoix's mother worked in the processing
side of the operation, helping smelt base metals in zero

gravity furnaces, while her father worked in sales to other races.

Sighing, Agnoix came face to face with the reality that her life would fit into the machinery that is Vao Station, no matter her ideals and interests.

"Maybe I should just listen to Mom and yield to proper Xik'en tradition, be a cog in the machine. It was here before me and will be here long after I'm gone," Agnoix said, her voice forlorn and without hope, just as Cassidy Cane's fingers dragged across the outside of the glass window.

***

For a moment time stood still for Agnoix, until what she was seeing registered in her reptilian brain. Then a lifetime of existence on a fragile mining complex amid a hazardous asteroid belt kicked in.

"Help, I need help!" Agnoix yelled, her cry reverberating down the narrow hall as she rushed towards the nearest life station, her costume flapping in her haste.

Built into the outer walls of the mining complex, life stations resembled round blisters that jutted out from its metal surface, like moles on the body of the space station. They allowed an individual to see along the exterior walls of the complex better, to aid in rescue of distressed ships and people working in the void of space. Dashing into the life station, Agnoix smashed the huge yellow button set into the facade, releasing the pistol grips of the bubble gun. Ignoring the flashing lights and siren that hitting the button had activated, Agnoix gripped the dual pistol grips of the bubble gun and a screen flashed to life. Cross-hairs bobbed and weaved as they mirrored her movements of the grips.

Shaking with adrenaline, Agnoix struggled to bring the cross-hairs on the screen to overlap with the shrinking form she saw through the window. With the sensors unable to detect a warm body to lock onto, Agnoix made her best guess and fired. Her sharp talons depressed the buttons on top of the pistol grips, firing the bubble gun.

From some place beneath her, a flashing disk shot out towards the body and sailed past without making contact, missing it by several meters.

"Come on, you can do this, every child has shot a bubble gun," Agnoix said to herself as she pushed her mask off her face. Adjusting her aim, she enhanced the view screen to maximum and discharged the bubble gun again. The flashing disk shot out and, this time, the viewscreen strobed yellow, saying that it had struck something and was returning to the life station.

Jumping in excitement, Agnoix almost didn't hear the computerized voice instructing her to exit the life station since a rescue was ongoing. Her tail striking the wall as she skipped out of the life station, Agnoix hurried to comply. When the sensors read that it was empty, the entire thing rotated outward. The interior of the tiny life station Agnoix was standing in moments ago, was now out in the void of space. And the protruding window was poking into the gallery corridor, oblivious to the strobing lights, sirens, and computerized voice of the life station.

It stated that she should remain on the scene of the rescue in progress, and that emergency staff had been dispatched. Agnoix watched as the 'bubble' and its occupant grew closer.

Seconds that felt like hours passed. The 'bubble,' a portable life-saving sphere used when there wasn't time to don a spacesuit, glided into the life station. The flashing disk, the 'cap' of the life-saving air bubble, connected with the interior of the window where Agnoix had stood, aiming her cross-hairs, minutes ago.

Agnoix couldn't get an unobstructed view of the being within the 'bubble.' The warm air being generated by the flashing disk had formed a thick layer of vapor within it, creating a sealed environment. As the life station received the rescue bubble, Agnoix felt the vibration through the metal floor. As the life station rotated back to its regular configuration, with the 'bubble' now inside the safety of the mining complex, Agnoix rushed towards it.

It's task completed, the flashing disk shut down and burst the life-saving bubble. Hot, moist air, with the faintest scent of disinfectant, flowed towards the young Xik'en. She saw the shadow of a body roll towards her out of the fog, its scale-less hand coming to rest on her foot.

Looking down at Cassidy, Agnoix, her voice on the edge of panic, yelled: "By all the ancestors, it's a mammal!"

CHAPTER FIVE

Scared and also intrigued by the alien *creature*, Agnoix leaned closer to the mammal. Tales of such Bogeyman were used to scare Xik'en children when they didn't eat all their supper or finish their homework. Agnoix knew that sentient mammals frequented the mining complex to trade for the metals produced here. Mammals were isolated and quarantined from all common areas, so that the ordinary work force and citizens of the complex never met them, nor risked being tainted.

Agnoix reached out a shaky talon and nudged the mammal. Feeling the chill radiating off of its skin, a small moan told the young Xik'en that the mammal was still alive.

"Great, you're alive... whatever you are," Agnoix said as she struggled to understand the strange clothes, hair -- *by all the ancestors, hair is ugly* -- and body shape of the warm-blood, and that's when she decided: *I can't leave you here. There are so many questions I want to ask about you, your world, your life.*

Looking around at the flashing lights and sirens, Agnoix realized what she'd done, activating the life station.

Her actions had no doubt caused several control boards in the mining complex base of operations to light up as if there was a magnetic storm. Agnoix knew she couldn't allow this mammal to fall into the talons of the stations security. She wanted to learn more about the mysterious alien: where it came from, and how it got into space without a suit. Something clicked within the young Xik'en, and she knelt beside Cassidy.

"Likely, they would throw you into a cage and charge you with trespassing, sabotage, or worse. I can't let that happen, at least not until you can speak on your own behalf, but that means we have to hide and quick."

This brilliant piece of reasoning only got Agnoix another moan from the warm-blood. Cassidy's eyes fluttered, her cheeks pulling in as she struggled to breathe through the face mask, no longer receiving oxygen from an empty tank.

"You can't die now, I just rescued you," Agnoix said, wishing that she was doing the proper thing as she pulled aside the oxygen mask, allowing Cassidy to inhale the foreign air. There were gasps that turned into great gulps of breathing, and Agnoix watched as colour appeared on the mammal's skin, her blood warming and oxygenating. Convinced that she did the correct thing, she searched for a place to hide them both, knowing that emergency personnel would be there at any moment.

With the central hallways away from the gallery likely to have Xik'ens rushing down them, Agnoix spied a tucked away maintenance area. Little better than a custodian's closet, but Agnoix decided it was for the best. Grabbing the tiny emergency kit from the life station and gripping it with her prehensile tail, Agnoix hesitated a second, looking at the alien at her feet. Staring at the warm-blood, her mind swirled with fear and excitement. The young Xik'en hooked her talons under the armpits of the strange mammal and pulled. Trying not to think that she was touching a horror of her culture, Agnoix dragged Cassidy towards the room, even as she heard steps running over the sirens.

Heedless of any suffering she might cause to Cassidy, Agnoix tugged her to the door of the custodian's closet. With little grace, she rolled Cassidy inside and stumbled after her, dragging the door closed just as she saw station personnel turn into the corridor.

The door to the janitor's closet jammed a talons width from closing. Agnoix looked down to see that the mammal's foot covering -- *why cover your feet?* -- was jamming the door. Leaning over the warm-blood, her nostrils drawing in the foreign scent, she reached to tug it clear. As she did so, she saw a running pair of Xik'en security guards with stun sticks in hand stop in front of the life station.

Frozen in place, squatting in the pitch black closet, Agnoix felt the soft breathing of the alien against her scales. Agnoix watched as the security guards holstered their stun sticks and rebooted the life station. It surprised Agnoix how intensely her heart was beating. She wondered if the guards would have been able to hear it, when the piercing siren of the alarm was shut off.

Leaning her head as close to the door gap as possible, Agnoix could hear the two guards outside.

"Control, this is Krolzan. No visual emergency at life station 42, don't bother sending medical aid. Unit reset, we're investigating," a mature female voice reported.

A communicator hissed. "Acknowledged. Awaiting a final report."

Another voice uttered, young to Agnoix's ears: "Do you... do you think it was a spirit called here on Sastreni? My Father's elder used to tell me tales of souls who visited on tonight; some appeared to help, some to harm."

Agnoix could pick out the agitation in Krolzan's tone, so similar to that of her own mother. "Tuds, if you wish to go on working security, learn and think for yourself. What is tonight, Tuds?"

"Ah... Sastreni, Sergeant Krolzan."

"That's right, and what did you do on your last Sastreni?"

"Attended a remembrance service to pay tribute to our ancestors," Tuds replied.

"Of course you did. Okay, let me ask it another way. What did your peers do that night while you were at the service?"

"Oh, you mean the cool kids. They partied, played practical jokes on people and caused mischief with security... I follow you now Sergeant, you think young Xik'ens activated the life station as a prank?"

"There's no dullness to your scales tonight is there, Tuds," Krolzan said in a deadpan tone, as she switched on her communicator.

"Krolzan to Control. Confirmed no emergency at this life station, likely just kids out causing trouble on Sastreni. Do you wish us to continue our investigation?"

The communicator crackled and an annoyed voice answered. "Negative Krolzan. Haul tail to the food court in section seven. A group of young Xik'ens, their leader dressed as Tox'eix, are creating a disturbance, more petty vandalism and lewd behaviour."

Thank you, Axaik, for once you did me a favour, Agnoix thought, as the pair of security officers hurried off, their stun sticks grasped in their strong talons.

Able to breathe a sigh of relief, Agnoix pulled the foot of the mammal out of the door, closed it, and turned on the light in the custodian's closet.

Climbing off the odd smelling mammal, Agnoix got her first clear view of Cassidy.

"Ugly aren't you?" Agnoix said as she struggled to make the unconscious woman comfortable. Realizing that Cassidy's extremities were as cold as ice and that the slight pulsing of her neck was becoming feeble, Agnoix felt her own stomach go cold.

"Please don't die!" Agnoix exclaimed, then tore open the emergency kit, flinging the contents throughout the cramped closet -- sanitation supplies falling from racks. While yet a youngster in the minds of Xik'en society, Agnoix and all like her that grew up on the space station were educated in basic first aid and emergency procedures. "Yeah, but the broadcasts on the transit tubes never mentioned what to do with frozen mammals," Agnoix muttered to herself as she grasped the injector for 'cold space'.

Bending down until her snout was almost touching Cassidy's ear, Agnoix whispered: "I'm giving you an injection, okay? I don't know what it will do for a warm-blood like you. They created it for Xik'ens when there is a rupture in the mining complex. Sorry if this hurts." And with a moment's reluctance, Agnoix placed the tip of the injector against Cassidy's neck. The soft hiss of the injector let her know that she had administered the medicine.

The result was instantaneous. Cassidy thrashed, drumming her heels against the floor of the closet. One of Cassidy's arms lashed out, knocking over a cleaning wand, and the other slapped Agnoix in the skull, making her tumble backward. Shaking her head to clear her vision, Agnoix climbed atop Cassidy and held her down. The talons of the Xik'en youth ripped the fabric of Cassidy's clothes, scratching the skin and drawing blood.

Cassidy made several cries, and her eyes rolled up into her sockets until only the whites showed. However, over minutes, Cassidy's struggles lessened and an intense glow radiated through her skin that Agnoix hoped meant good news.

As the alien creature's struggles lessened, Agnoix climbed off, confirming in her own mind that the 'cold space' had reversed the effects of being exposed to the vacuum of space. With the immediate danger behind them, Agnoix's curiosity took over, and she slid herself closer to the alien for a decent look.

"You're fragile, aren't you?" Agnoix said as she examined Cassidy. "Delicate skin, no scales to protect you, so you wear many layers of clothes. I bet your sense of smell is terrible with a snout so ugly and stunted as that, and why are your teeth blunt? Do you grind your food between your jaws? A very inefficient design. How your species attained space is beyond me, or are you a stowaway? I just wish I had my sketchbook to capture this!"

Maybe it was Agnoix's excited tone of voice, or that

the stimulant had worked, but Cassidy's eyes opened wide at the creature leaning over of her.

***

Mother was right, mammals are dangerous! Look at the fury in its ugly face, how it grabbed for a weapon, Agnoix thought to herself as she struggled to grasp the handle of the custodian's closet, her flee to safety monopolizing her thoughts.

"Stop it you twit, do you expect you'd be in any better condition if you were just recovered from the void and woke up in a strange place?" Agnoix chastised herself. "You're letting your racial bias show; don't judge without evidence."

With deliberate effort, Agnoix released the door handle and turned towards the alien mammal.

I've never seen this species of warm-blood before, just images on a screen. It's probably as terrified of me as I am of it, Agnoix thought as she regarded Cassidy. She lifted her taloned hand. "My name is Agnoix, are you feeling okay?"

She repeated herself several times and attempted the gentlest voice she could. It worked because she watched as the mammal lowered the window cleaner wand, picked up as a weapon, and leaned it against the wall, still within easy reach.

Straightening to its full stature, less than Agnoix's own, the mammal tapped its chest with a blunt and ugly finger and answered: "Cassidy."

"Well, at least it can communicate. That's something at least," Agnoix said, and the mammal turned its head sideways as if struggling to understand.

"I appreciate you can't understand me, warm-blood, but I have something that I hope will work," Agnoix said as she reached her hand into the pleats of her costume, causing the mammal to reach for its weapon.

"Please don't. I'm getting something to help us communicate, okay?" Agnoix whispered, and the mammal stopped reaching for the window cleaner. Pulling her Branch of Languages from her robe -- the golden nanotech wires cradling slivers of green Vao stones -- Agnoix didn't see any shock of recognition from the alien mammal. Placing the branch against the right side of her scaled jaw, Agnoix showed Cassidy how the intelligent device weaved itself along her jawline, around her ear, and stopped at the crest of her head.

Things were about to get interesting.

CHAPTER SIX

Cassidy's eyes widened in confusion as she watched the dinosaur creature reach into its clothing and draw forth a piece of the very crystal Gamgee sent her to find.

Her shock continued as the alien laid the jeweled necklace against its scaled face, and it coiled itself around the skull as if it were alive.

The final straw was when the alien dinosaur held out the necklace to Cassidy. What was worse was that the device itself appeared to reach out to her. Trauma of the past several minutes took its toll. Her knees weakened, she slumped down the wall, and passed out.

Reality returned to Cassidy much sharper than it appeared the first time, but it was no less disconcerting.

The alien had stretched out her legs to make Cassidy as comfortable as she could, and had even put her makeshift weapon beside her hand.

The desire to take up the weapon was powerful, but Cassidy pushed it from her thoughts. Instead, she focused her mind on the alien sitting on its haunches, watching her, its scaled tail flicking like a cat's.

Think Cassidy, apply your training instead of acting out of fear. You've been in strange and perilous places before -- even though this must be near the top of the list.

Okay, I'm lying in a tiny room with an intelligent reptile. Focus on that.

Cassidy took several deep breaths as she slipped back into her training as an anthropologist and cataloged what she saw in front of her.

She did her best to remain objective in her analysis, and wished she dared risk digging out her notebook.

Bipedal with a prehensile tail since its operating it as a third hand to carry an empty box, the contents strewn throughout this room. More of a closet, maybe? Doesn't feel like a home or a hospital.

Focus! Concentrate on the alien, Cassidy.

It's tough to know, since I'm prone and the alien is squatting, but I'd estimate it's at least my height when standing, maybe taller. It has the typical number of limbs and fingers and toes, though what I consider normal in this situation I don't know.

Protruding snout, broad nasal opening, a mouth full of tiny sharp teeth and a tongue that flicks out every few moments. It reminds me of how a snake samples the air, drawing a sample into its mouth and its vomeronasal system.

Large round eyes with lavender pupils, exquisite eyes to be honest. They rest on the front of the face rather than the side, which denotes a predator verses prey ancestry, analogous to humans.

Its scales are like tarnished bronze, like the jewelry I helped excavate from that Roman-Britain dig a couple seasons back. Its outfit is baffling, it's a series of robes striped in yellow and blue, though the colours appear to be painted on -- and not skillful, if

I'm being fair. Strapped over that is armour, but it's homemade or ceremonial and not for combat. I can say the same for its weapon, a fork on one end, and a hook on the other, either a prop or a toy. My best guess is that the attire is for ceremonial rather than everyday use.

Years in the field, exposed to various cultures, had allowed Cassidy to catalogue people and items as second nature, and she did so again in moments.

Relying on her abilities and feelings, Cassidy sensed that while this alien looked fearsome, it didn't mean her immediate harm.

Pleased that her hand had stopped shaking, Cassidy reached out for the necklace.

Alien talons brushed against Cassidy's palm, but she didn't allow herself to jerk away.

Holding her breath, Cassidy lifted the piece of alien jewelry up to her face, and she felt it become alive.

Moving like a snake, it slipped along Cassidy's jawline, and its "head" disappeared into the hair above her right ear. The living wire followed her jawline on one end, while the other weaved its way into her braided hair.

A comfortable warmth replaced the tingle, and a thought occurred to Cassidy. The pauses and word groups of the alien language reminded her of the Khoisan languages of southern Africa with their clicks. *I wonder if any member of these aliens has ever been to Earth in the past? I must attempt to research this. The results could open up a new branch of linguistics.*

Cassidy tested her theory. Taking a deep breath with lungs that minutes before were about to breathe nothing but the cold of space, she said: "Is this thing working?"

A warm tingling raced along her scalp. "This is amazing," Cassidy said, only to see disappointment on the female reptile's face.

I don't understand it... I know it's alien technology, but I'm sure it should work, she thought, as she allowed her fingers to glide along the golden wire cradling the right side of her head.

Fool, you should head back to school when this is all over, Cassidy chided herself, as she beckoned Agnoix to remove the device. Once it was free, Cassidy patted the left side of her face, and while the young Xik'en shook her head and said something in her own language, she did as Cassidy requested and repeated the ritual on the left side of Cassidy's face.

Once she felt the warm tingling along her scalp again, Cassidy said: "How about now?" and Agnoix clapped her taloned hands happily in response.

"I can understand you!" Agnoix said.

No, that isn't right. If I focus, I can still hear Agnoix's alien speech patterns, but what she says is an echo in my mind. This alien device must be in direct contact with my brain.

The mere thought of what this piece of alien technology might do to her brain nearly caused a panic attack, so Cassidy hurried to distract herself.

"In humans, the language portion of our brain is on the left side," she said, tapping the left side of her head. "That's why it didn't work the first time, I bet."

***

Relieved that the mammal seemed unhurt and relaxed after donning the Branch of Languages, Agnoix forced her heart to slow down and her conflicting instincts to flee, with Agnoix standing firm.

Tapping her breast once again with her talon, Agnoix said: "My name is Agnoix, what is your name?"

Agnoix smiled as she watched Cassidy shudder, remembering the tingling sensations as the Branch of Languages attached to its users speech centre.

The warm-blood's tone of voice was deeper than most intelligent species. Its tiny mouth mispronounced some words, but Agnoix learned that the mammal called itself Cassidy Cane and came from a place or planet called Earth.

While many of the terms the mammal used were unfamiliar to Agnoix, making her blink in confusion more than once, she was able to gather that this mammal -- correction, 'human' -- was here on a voyage of exploration in general, and after ARC crystals in specific. The ARC crystals, Cassidy Cane explained, look like larger versions of the stones in her Branch of Languages, and Agnoix could understand why.

The Vao stones were one of the major exports from this mining station. While the base and precious metals, mined and refined from the asteroid belt, made up the shear bulk of the material that went through this mining complex, the Vao stones were the most expensive.

Xik'en scientists had a complicated means of describing their ability, but all that Agnoix knew was that they allowed the Xik'en Interstellar Empire instantaneous communication across space. That communication was the primary reason that their reach and control was so vast.

Pieces of the Vao stones used with base level intelligent nanotechnology could create the Branches of Languages. These personal translation devices were a staple on the mining stations and other places where many races coexisted under one roof.

Agnoix was grateful for the one her parents had gifted her on her last hatching day. Her mother hadn't want to give Agnoix such a tool, fearing that it would encourage her willful daughter to mingle with more outside their own species.

"Mother! I'd forgotten, it must be way past the time I promised to be home. I don't know what to do."

CHAPTER SEVEN

Much of what the alien -- *make that Xik'en*, Cassidy corrected herself -- said was confusing.

The alien language was high-pitched, like a parrot trained to speak, but the alien device connected to her skull translated the words for Cassidy.

The speech patterns were like a nervous teenager on a first date, speaking without thinking. *Well, from what this Agnoix says, I gather she is like a teenager.*

Reviewing what she'd learned, Cassidy found herself at a loss for words.

She was on a mining station that doubled as a trade port for a vast reptilian empire, inhabited by the Xik'ens.

Cassidy found out she was lucky that Agnoix had saved her, because her culture saw warm-bloods -- mammals -- as bogeymen, a barbaric sub-intelligent species prone to violence and cannibalism.

Doing her best to force the visuals of that out of her mind, Cassidy tried to straighten out the rest of the knowledge that Agnoix had supplied her with.

Tonight was Sastreni, which appeared to be a cross between Halloween and Founder's Day in Xik'en culture. The youth dressed up as the founders of their culture, though Cassidy wasn't clear on if they were mythical characters or actual people. Agnoix was dressed up as 'Brauxel', which -- as far as Cassidy could determine -- was a Joan of Arc type personality, and not very mainstream.

When Agnoix got to the part of the narrative about how her brother, Axaik, had abandoned her to attend a party with his buddies, Cassidy spoke up.

"I have siblings, sisters of my own, and I understand what you mean. Many times my sisters ditched me to hang out in the mall or go for a ride with their friends when they had promised to do something with me." Realizing that some of her language and terms were confusing the younger Xik'en, she clarified: "Sorry, I just mean I understand where you're coming from. Can we start fresh?" She stuck out her hand. "I'm Cassidy, thank you for saving my life, and I'd like to be your friend."

***

Much of what the mammal -- no. Correct that, her name is Cassidy, Agnoix thought to herself. Much of what Cassidy is saying makes little sense, but I don't think she means me or the mining complex any harm.

Doing her best to explain herself without sounding like a child, Cassidy startled Agnoix when she reached out an open palm in friendship.

Stretching towards Cassidy, Agnoix reached out her own hand and placed it palm to palm against the human's, and did her best not to jump when Cassidy wrapped her fingers around her hand and shook it. Puzzled by the odd ritual, Agnoix gripped Cassidy's hand and, likewise, shook it.

"So what now, you can't stay here?"

***

Doing her best not to grimace as Agnoix's taloned hand almost crushed hers, Cassidy responded to the young Xik'en. "I think my priority is to figure out a way home, but I'd also love to pick up a sample of these Vao stones for Doctor Gamgee back home. This is your home, do you have any suggestions?"

Touched that this adult, even if it was a mammal, was seeking her guidance, Agnoix considered. *I don't think Cassidy is conscious how much danger she is in. An unlisted mammal on a Xik'en space station and inside the alien free zone. If she's lucky, she'll get roughed by security, but if the wrong people find her it's the airlock for sure, and this time without a breathing mask.*

Counting on the differences in their societies to conceal any doubt, Agnoix thought, and the hint of a solution began to take hold.

"I think I might have an idea that fits both your goals, but it will involve some risk. I have one condition though: you must take me as far as this portal in the asteroid belt. I want to see it." Even while being translated through the Branch of Languages, Agnoix's excitement came through. "Are you agreeable?" Agnoix asked.

"Agreeable? Heck yes. Risk is my middle name," Cassidy said. Observing the bewildered expression on Agnoix's face, Cassidy tried to explain. "Ah, it's an expression where I'm from, it means that is acceptable."

I wonder if all humans are this strange, Agnoix thought to herself.

CHAPTER EIGHT

Agnoix couldn't believe her luck when Cassidy agreed to take her as far as the portal. Unknown to Cassidy, Agnoix planned on following Cassidy through, to explore this strange new world called Earth.

"But work comes first, as my mother would say," Agnoix began as she stepped backward to look upon the human. "And we have some work to do if we don't want you looking like a... a... warm-blood. Sorry."

Cassidy's blunt-toothed grin startled Agnoix -- *their teeth are so ugly* -- but she proceeded.

"We need to get you into a disguise..." Agnoix muttered, and started rooting around the custodian's closet to discover what she had available, as Cassidy watched her and grinned.

I'm certain she could snap me in two with no effort, and by her own admission she's not yet matured. I realize I've only known her for minutes, and maybe it's the lack of oxygen to my brain or that strange drug she injected me with, but I like the kid, Cassidy thought to herself. She then asked Agnoix: "So this Sastreni of yours sounds like our Halloween back home. We'd dress up as superheroes or witches or goblins and go door to door in the neighbourhood saying 'Trick or Treat'. We always got treats."

The young Xik'en rummaged through the custodian's closet, putting material into a heap. The heap contained the contents of the emergency kit, a disposable sanitation bio-suit, and other items that might be useful in disguising the human.

"So you dressed up as well? And did this Treat-tricking?" Agnoix asked.

"It's called 'Trick or Treating'. But yeah, I would do it with my sisters, though more than once they ditched me to go off with their friends, not unlike what your brother did. I'm sorry, it sucks, I know."

Agnoix could figure out the essentials of what Cassidy said, and suspected that 'sucking' is something bad. "So what was your costume?" Agnoix asked as she realized that all her hard work needed major repairs after its ordeal tonight.

"I mostly went with classic monsters, even though my Mom always wanted to dress me as a princess. I enjoyed dressing up as the Mummy, a witch, and even one year as the headless horseman," Cassidy said, and at Agnoix's puzzled expression elaborated: "Ah... I'll explain it another time. Wait, I have an idea. What about a ghost?"

"The ghost of whom?" asked Agnoix.

"Does it matter? Can't it be a generic ghost? Does it have to be a specific individual?"

"Well, in Xik'en society, we honour our notable founders with our Sastreni costumes, but your idea should work!" Agnoix said, starting to pick out different pieces from her pile.

"Here," Agnoix said, thrusting the bio-suit at Cassidy. "Put this on. It will cover your... un-Xik'enness." The complete absurdity of the situation struck the two of them, and they both laughed. Struggling to control herself, Agnoix said: "We must be quiet in case anyone passes the hall."

Still chuckling, the pair did their best to get Cassidy into the bio-suit, but the void where a Xik'en would stick out their tail stumped them for a moment. "I have it," hissed Agnoix, as she attempted to contain her laughter. "Here, stick the window cleaner in the belt of your pants and it should fill in the tail section." Picking up the tool that Cassidy had meant to use as a weapon minutes before, Agnoix helped Cassidy fit it as she had proposed. She shook her head. "I do not understand how you walk around without a tail. I'd think you would fall on your face, being unable to balance."

This started the laughter between them anew but, with a force of will, the two stopped and finished Cassidy's costume.

They sealed her up in the janitor's disposable bio-suit, fake tail and all. Agnoix took the emergency heating blanket from the first aid kit, which she kicked herself for forgetting about when she could have used it, and passed it to the human. Cassidy used her pocket knife to cut two neat eye-holes in the blanket. They draped the blanket over her and -- using orange flapping tape from her field kit to secure it around her neck and arms -- she presented herself for inspection.

"Well..." Agnoix said as she looked Cassidy up and down. "It is a unique costume. No one will wonder what species you are in this: rather they'll question your mental abilities." Seeing her new friend slump, she hastened to add, "But what do they know? I think this ghost costume could take off. Now we just need to make sure no one talks to you. Your odd voice will make people curious," Agnoix said, then slapped her tail against the floor in agitation. "I'm such a mammal sometimes," she cursed. She stopped and looked at Cassidy, her eyes wide. "Sorry, it's just a figure of speech. I just forgot something. We need to get this blanket off you for a minute. You don't have a proper snout."

Agnoix grabbed Cassidy's depleted breathing mask. Disconnecting the mask from the hose and tank, Agnoix helped Cassidy drape the mask around the Branch of Languages. Within the blanket, Cassidy would have the shape of a Xik'en face as long as no one looked too close.

"I've never heard of another race of beings such as you. I'm not allowed to study alien biology as much as I would like; they forbid many of those records to Xik'ens outside of scholarship."

"Well, you're my first alien friend, so that makes us even," Cassidy replied, and could see that her vow of friendship had touched the youthful girl.

Grinning in pleasure, Agnoix tried to maintain her cool and turned her attention back to the matter at hand.

"I'm glad it works... friend Cassidy, but we should get you covered again and start moving to the mining bay before shift change."

Together, the two got Cassidy under the blanket again and got Agnoix's costume back into a semblance of order. A liberal amount of wound glue from the emergency kit and flagging tape from Cassidy's pack got the job done.

Their faces concealed, the two nodded at each other and turned to the door of the custodian's closet.

Agnoix reached out and slid the door open a fraction, and realized that the light within the room could easily highlight the pair to anybody in the hallway.

"The light -- turn it off Cassidy," Agnoix hissed.

Cassidy couldn't help but notice how the Xik'en's tongue curled as she spoke and was disappointed the translation device didn't add extra "sss" sounds like it would in a B-Movie.

"The Light!" Agnoix said again, and Cassidy shook the errant thought from her mind and did as she was asked. Figuring out the switch wasn't unduly hard. She just needed to place her finger within a socket and turn it, until the only light within the closet was that coming in from the outside.

After several minutes of watching, with her entire view of the mining complex a narrow slice of empty hall seen over Agnoix's shoulder, Cassidy was about to ask if there was a problem. Before she could, Agnoix slid the door open and stepped into the hallway, waving for her new friend to follow her.

***

With a tentative step, Cassidy walked into the gallery hallway of the mining complex and took in the spectacular view of being inside an alien space station.

Ignoring Agnoix's pleas to follow her, Cassidy walked, spellbound, to the window, her fake tail swinging behind her as if it had a mind of its own.

Standing in front of the immense window, her heavy breathing ruffling the sheet over her face, Cassidy watched the asteroid belt of the Vao system before her.

Like a bag of glass marbles tossed in a gravel driveway, the glistening rocks tumbled around the sky of the mining complex, highlighted by an exquisite shine.

"It's breathtaking," Cassidy said, as she placed her palms against the window. It was as if she were yearning to seize one of the asteroids.

Coming up behind her friend, Agnoix looked upon the asteroid belt that had been her home for her whole life through the eyes of the human, and saw it anew.

"You're right, it is, isn't it?" Agnoix said. "The glow is the super fine dust that is being highlighted by the rays of the sun. During solar storms it lights up like fireworks."

Touching her friend's arm, Agnoix said: "Cassidy, we need to move." With a slight tug, she drew the woman along with her, away from the mesmerizing view.

While drawing her attention away from the spectacular view outside the mining complex window, Cassidy couldn't help but wonder aloud: "Why don't the asteroids hit the station?"

"Magnets," Agnoix answered.

"Magnets? You can't be serious," Cassidy said. She pushed herself to keep up with the Xik'en youth and take in as much of the detail of the space station as she could through her costume's eye holes.

"The mining complex is enveloped by a field of magnetized orbs, which operate as a security blanket around the complex, and it cushions against any strike. Any asteroids too massive or without sufficient iron content are steered away by the mining pods," Agnoix said to ease any fears. *She is only a mammal,* Agnoix thought to herself, and then was ashamed that her racial bias came so easily to her. She hastened to explain: "There hasn't been a strike on the complex since my Father's Father's time, and that was during a terrible solar storm before they upgraded the magnetic shield. You're safe here, Cassidy."

Agnoix saw the shadow of a smile reflected in the eyes peering at her through the holes of the costume.

"I know I am Agnoix, but like you said, we should go."

Cassidy turned away from one wonder to take in another.

From Cassidy's point of view, the Xik'en mining complex was too bright for her eyes. The pounding headache behind her eyes attested to that, though Cassidy did her best to catalogue the home of Agnoix's people.

The light level is probably the same on their native world; what their eyes have evolved to accept. That must go for the atmosphere, too. Whether it's the alien drug Agnoix injected me with causing me to feel light-headed or not, but I'd say the oxygen content is higher than what I'm used to. That goes double for the mugginess, Cassidy thought to herself, as she tried to scratch her back where the thin trickle of sweat was forming.

But even that discomfort couldn't distract Cassidy from her experience.

The mining station feels very organic to me. The tunnels are rounded and they raise, dip and curl as if formed by water over thousands of years. Along the walls are shelves, I guess, and each has various plants and mosses growing within them, whether it's for oxygen production, simple decoration, or both I don't know. I must ask Agnoix.

You're so busy gawking around that you neglected your primary source. Who knows how much time we have together? I need to make the most of it.

"Agnoix," Cassidy began, and watched as her friend peeked around the curving tunnel to determine if anyone else was close.

The coast clear, the young Xik'en hurried back to her new friend. "Yes, is there a problem? Do you smell someone behind us?"

"No, nothing like that. I just wanted you to tell me a little about yourself and your people while we have the time," Cassidy replied.

And while Agnoix understood the peril better than Cassidy, the adolescent Xik'en girl also wanted to hear something of the world from which Cassidy was from.

"Okay, Cassidy, but let's go back and forth. I'm curious about your world too," Agnoix said, motioning for Cassidy to follow her. They continued slinking down the tunnel.

"It's hard to know where to start," Agnoix began. "The Xik'en are an ancient and prideful race; our reach is vast, though most of us don't like to travel far unless it's necessary. Though I've always wanted to stand beneath a true sky."

Looking behind her to make certain there wasn't anybody near them, Cassidy turned back to Agnoix. "You mean you've never been outside before? Isn't there a Xik'en home planet?"

"Oh there is, it's called 'Xik'en', very original isn't it?"

Agnoix puffed her cheeks in amusement. "I might go there someday. It's a pilgrimage every Xik'en is supposed to do once in their life, but I'd rather travel to an alien planet like yours. What's 'Human' like, Cassidy?"

Through the sheet over her face, Cassidy could conceal her grin. "Earth is the name of my home world, and we're nowhere near your level of technology. My people haven't traveled farther than our moon."

Hearing movement and seeing shadows flicker in the tunnel up ahead, Agnoix pushed Cassidy back a step so they could wait and see if they needed to hide. While waiting, Agnoix continued in a soft tone: "I don't understand. Then how did you end up outside? Were you a stowaway onboard a ship? Are you a lawbreaker on the run from the authorities?" The young Xik'en's lavender eyes grew wide.

"Ha ha, nothing like that, Agnoix, I promise. A portal brought me here. I work with a scientist named Gamgee, and I am exploring these portals for him. Each one leads me to a unique dimension: some are like my world's history, and others are alien like here. I flew my airplane -- that's an atmospheric craft -- through a portal and found myself amid your asteroid belt. If you hadn't rescued me when you did, your miners would have discovered my frozen body someday. I didn't expect to end up in space."

With a tale that outlandish, I'm inclined to believe her, Agnoix thought to herself. *I mean there are a hundred other stories that would almost make sense. She jumped ship, tossed out an airlock in the quarantine zone. Or even pirates trying to steal asteroids, but portals and alternative dimensions?*

"Scale rot," Agnoix cursed. "I believe you, Cassidy,

though if anybody else were to hear that story, especially from a mammal... I mean 'human', they would detain you in a flash."

"Then I guess we had better not get caught," Cassidy said, and put a hand on the Xik'en's shoulder just as a new voice asked: "What do we have here, my fellow Sastreni celebrants!"

CHAPTER NINE

Oh please, don't let it be him... Agnoix prayed, even as she looked past Cassidy and saw her brother Axaik and a crowd of his peers -- all dressed in their Sastreni costumes -- walking towards them.

"Spread out, my fellow revelers; don't let them slide down some hole like the mammal loving scum they are," Axaik hissed, and before either Agnoix or Cassidy could act, the group of nine nearly-mature Xik'ens fanned out in a half circle to block the two friends from fleeing.

Axaik handed off his beverage container, which smelled like rubbing alcohol to Cassidy's nose, to a fellow costumed Xik'en and walked towards his sister, who had placed herself in front of Cassidy.

"I'm right aren't I?" Axaik reached out a taloned finger and poked Cassidy in the chest, hard, causing her to inhale sharply. "Only a stinking mammal lover would hang around with my sister. The sister that everyone says is so smart and could do grand things if she just applied herself like a proper Xik'en."

"That's right, my friends," Axaik said over his shoulder, wobbling on his feet. "The disappointment in the family gets all the attention while I work hard, do all I'm asked. Apprenticed to the Trading Guild in some backwater station away from you fine reptiles."

"Axaik, you're drunk. How did you get Grove juice? That's forbidden outside of official celebrations," Agnoix said, shoving her brother's hand aside and directing his attention away from Cassidy.

"Forbidden!" Axaik roared, and his friends echoed the laughter.

They raised their own containers of the alcoholic beverage, several of them staggering on their feet. One even fell over, and needed help to stand again.

"Nothing is forbidden on Sastreni to those who have connections. You're not the only one interested in the aliens that come through this station. For the right amount of credits, a smart Xik'en can get anything he wants."

"And what will mother say when she finds out that you have been drinking Grove juice?" Agnoix threatened her older brother, then realized that might have been a mistake, as his eyes narrowed and his lips retracted, showing pointed teeth.

Tilting his head to the side, Agnoix lashed out with lightening speed and grabbed each of the women, his talons ripping into their costumes. "My mother will not find out about this, will she gang? Not if these two mammal lovers spend some time locked in a storage cage." His alcohol laced breath assaulted them. "Spend a night away from home and Mom won't believe anything you say. Especially after I tell her how you slipped away from your older and caring brother, and myself and my hardworking Xik'en friends sacrificed our last Sastreni to look for you."

"Don't do this Axaik, I know we're not close but…"

Axaik interrupted by shaking them, the sound of ripping fabric getting louder. The front of the reserve parachute strapped to Cassidy's chest poked out.

Releasing his hold, Axaik pushed his sister aside. His friends grabbed her when she struggled to escape.

"You haven't said a word. Do I know you?" Axaik asked as he flicked a tattered piece of Cassidy's makeshift costume. "And what are you supposed to be, anyway? That's not like any Sastreni costume I've seen before."

"You leave her alone, Axaik, she's just a friend, someone new to the station, you just haven't met her yet."

"I'm sure if you had gotten a friend I would have heard about it," Axaik said, focusing all his attention on the costumed Cassidy. "You're outnumbered, and if you don't want to spend a night in a cold dark storage cage with my little sister then you better tell us who you are."

The Branch of Languages allowed her to speak and understand the Xik'en language, and Cassidy knew what was happening and decided that she didn't like Axaik.

Knocking his talon-tipped hand aside, Cassidy stood as straight as she could. And while she only reached Axaik's chin, her physical presence caused the drunken youth to take a step back, his weak laugh a poor mask for his hesitation.

"You want to know who and what I am? Then let me show you!" Cassidy exclaimed, the genderless voice produced by the Branch of Languages making her words menacing. Cassidy gripped the bottom of the sheet and ripped it over her head.

Ignoring the cry of "Stop" from Agnoix, Cassidy flung the costume aside. With her braided hair swinging, wide eyes, and sweat-covered face, Cassidy yelled: "I am Cassidy Cane, Explorer from the planet Earth: a warm-blooded mammal that wants nothing more than to grab as many Xik'ens as I can and eat them!" She then mock-lunged at Axaik.

Brain clouded with drink, stuck in a situation that wasn't going the way he'd planned, and faced with the bogeyman his race had feared since they left their home world, Axaik did the only thing he could. He screamed in terror, then turned to flee.

Like a stampede, the other scared and confused youths reacted on their most primal levels and followed suit. Stumbling over each other while yelling and screaming in fear, they clawed their way down the hallway, heedless of the harm done to their fellows.

Dusting her hands off, a wide smile on her face, Cassidy leaned down, picked up one of the dropped containers, and smelled the alcoholic contents. She scrunched up her nose. "What is this stuff? Smells like something my father used to clean paint brushes."

Not getting an answer, Cassidy turned and saw Agnoix staring dumbstruck at her.

"Agnoix? Are you okay?" Cassidy said, taking a step towards her friend, and the young Xik'en jumped backward.

They're told their entire lives that warm-bloods are the devils of their culture and you used that against your friend. Likely the only person on this entire mining station that would have saved me and I do this. Why do I leap before I think? Cassidy thought to herself, sobering her mood. "I'm sorry, Agnoix, I wasn't serious about eating your brother or anyone. I was just trying to get them to leave us alone, and I wasn't thinking how it would turn out. I really am sorry, Agnoix. Can you forgive me?"

For several seconds a wide-eyed Agnoix just stared at Cassidy, as if fighting a war within herself. Should she do what her instincts were telling her, to run in fear just as her brother had, or should she stay with her strange new friend, the only friend she'd ever had?

A slight shiver went through Agnoix, and then the youthful Xik'en smiled. "I'm okay, Cassidy. I'm not ashamed to say that you nearly scared the scales off me. All I could think of was the monsters they threatened me with as a child, the ones I KNEW lived in my closet and came out at night." Looking at the uncovered human, Agnoix stepped forward. "We need to get you covered again. The yelling will bring trouble, no matter how late it is."

And as if called, the two women heard the sounds of clawed feet and loud voices racing towards them.

They did their best to get Cassidy's costume in order as a pair of Xik'en security guards rounded the corner. They saw the two costumed figures and hurried towards them, stun batons in their taloned fists.

With the focus being getting Cassidy back into her costume, Agnoix's own looks were in disarray. Her yellow and blue striped mask was on the ground. Realizing that she looked like a victim, Agnoix played into that, and waved at the security guards to hurry faster.

That simple gesture likely changed the whole outcome of the rest of the night.

Skidding to a stop in front of them, Agnoix found that it was the same two security guards who had responded to the life station when she had rescued Cassidy from outer space.

Focusing her attention on the older of the two, some tiny part of her brain remembered that her name was Krolzan. "Please, could you help two young Xik'en tormented and set upon by a group of older kids?" Agnoix said, hoping her innocent act came across as more believable than it sounded to her ears.

The older Xik'en looked a little ragged around the scales, but her eyes scanned the two youths in a professional matter before answering Agnoix. "What's going on here? It's getting a little late for you to still be out for Sastreni, isn't it?"

Forcing her eyes wide, Agnoix stuck her tongue out until it was just past her teeth, just as she'd seen the older girls do when looking for sympathy. She willed her tail to stop twitching in nervousness. "Myself and my friend..." She paused a second. "...*Caskad*, were out enjoying Sastreni when this group of older kids started teasing us and trying to destroy our costumes." Agnoix held her arms out wide to show her much abused costume as proof. "I won't want to get anyone in trouble, Officer, but a good Xik'en must do their duty and tell the truth, correct?"

"That's right, young miss," the young Xik'en named Tuds replied, even as he looked Agnoix up and down in an appreciative manner. "You and your friend should tell us everything." Tuds looked at Cassidy with fresh eyes.

Fearing discovery, Agnoix stepped towards Tuds and looked up at him. "I so want to be a dutiful citizen, so I'll tell you. I fear this group was drinking Grove juice. You could smell it on them, and look." Agnoix pointed to a container that Axaik and his friends had dropped in their rush to get away from Cassidy. "One of them dropped the smelly stuff when you scared them away." A flash of inspiration struck Agnoix, and she finished by saying: "They also were bragging about messing around and discharging an emergency life station earlier in the night, if that means anything."

"So that's who was responsible!" Krolzan growled, grabbing Tuds by the sleeve of his security uniform. "Come on, Tuds. I will have these trouble makers if it takes all night. This will be a Sastreni they won't forget." Krolzan turned to chase after Axaik and his friends, then stopped to looked at Agnoix and Cassidy. "You two are all right, aren't you? Do you need medical attention or an escort home? I could send for someone."

"We're fine," Agnoix blurted. "We're both okay. My friend and I are going right home like dutiful citizens, aren't we Caskad?"

Why did you do that?! They'll recognize the Branch of Languages and they'll discover Cassidy, Agnoix thought to herself.

Relief flooded through her when Cassidy didn't say a word, only nodded in agreement.

"See that you do. Come on, Tuds, we have work to do," Krolzan said, dragging a reluctant Tuds after her.

Once the sound of the security guards running faded out of earshot, Cassidy laughed. "Boys are the same no matter the dimension!"

Agnoix began shaking as she realized how close to

discovery they had been and how she had lied to the security guards. The young woman she had been this morning wouldn't recognize herself now.

"That scared me, Cassidy. I don't think you realize how close that was or what might have happened if they had caught you."

Walking over to her friend, Cassidy placed her hand on her shoulder. "Maybe I don't understand everything, but I know that you risked yourself to save me because you thought it was the right thing to do. Maybe lying isn't the best way to go about it, but at least this way your brother will get what's coming to him. I always sailed close to the wind when my friends were in danger."

Agnoix's mind raced as she visualized the problems that were awaiting her brother if the station's security personal found him and his friends. She found that it didn't bother her as much as she would have thought it would and chuckled, her tongue curling in joy.

"Okay, maybe you're right, Cassidy, but let's not do anymore of this 'wind sailing', I don't know how much more I can take." Agnoix picked up her fallen mask. "We still have the most dangerous part ahead of us. We need to sneak you into the mining area of the station and get you into a pod so we can get you home."

Cassidy stood up straight. "The ghosts of all Xik'ens are with us. Let's go."

Tugging on her mask, Agnoix smiled and led her friend deeper into the station.

CHAPTER TEN

Even Cassidy could tell that the station was changing. The beautiful flowing walls and tunnels of what she thought of as the residential area made way for plain square tunnels, with motorized carts of people whipping past.

The first couple of times the pair saw traffic or people moving around, Agnoix and Cassidy had tried to hide until they went past. That had soon proved impossible, and Cassidy had suggested something that was, for her, a tried-and-true course of action. "Act like you know what you're doing. Look straight ahead and walk with purpose, and most people will assume that you belong even if their instincts tell them otherwise. I can't tell you how many times that simple bluff has saved me grief."

Their bluff had worked; most of the Xik'ens did nothing but glance at them. But the increase in traffic made it hard for Cassidy to ask questions, fearing that someone would recognize the artificial voice of the Branch of Languages. Struggling with her words, Cassidy asked about the change in light levels.

The work and working life within this section of the

mining station didn't respect the clock. The lights shifted from a bright yellow to a bright orange, which Agnoix said signified the second of three stages of light on her home planet. Xik'en was a world that never went dark.

"The home world of my species, Xik'en, has one large primary star and two enormous gas giants. They're so close to the planet that they provide light upon its surface at all hours," Agnoix explained in a tone like someone repeating something from a class lecture. "The light of the primary is white, the gas giant Ilmone is orange, and Alnosie provides red. They reflect the three phases of a Xik'en's life, service and death."

She leaned towards Cassidy as a group of Xik'en, smelling of mineral dust, passed in the opposite direction. Agnoix whispered: "I wish we had more time to just get to know each other. Maybe you can tell me more of your human world while we hunt for your portal, Cassidy?"

I don't want to lie to Agnoix -- she's a friendly kid, nearly a grown woman herself. But I can't allow her to risk herself outside with me. I never really think of the risks I take, but allowing her to come into open space is just something I can't allow. I wonder if parenthood feels like this?

As the mineral processing workers passed, the dust following in their wake tickled Cassidy's nose, threatening to send her into a sneezing fit.

That brought the errant thought: "Do the Xik'en sneeze?", before she realized that she was avoiding answering Agnoix's question. "If there is time, my friend, I'll tell you whatever you want to know, I promise," Cassidy said, and the words soured her stomach. Upon the thought of her stomach, it grumbled.

"Are you hungry?" Agnoix asked. "I have some fruit leather that those who liked my Sastreni costume gave me."

"I'd try it, Agnoix. It must be better than those terrible molasses candies I got Trick or Treating as a kid. But until we get to a place where I can take off this costume, my stomach will just have to stay hungry," Cassidy said as she pointed to the large opening in the tunnel ahead of them. "Are we close?"

"Yes. We better not risk you talking anymore, just let me get us through the gates and then we can go from there."

I wish I was half as sure as I sounded. But Cassidy is relying on me to help get her home and I must do what I can if I want a chance to explore her world, Agnoix thought as she steered Cassidy away from the heavy traffic leading into the mining hub and towards the walkway that led to the checkpoint.

Agnoix watched as a series of automated work carts with equipment, supplies and personal each pulled up to the barrier, thumping her tail as she did.

Vehicles, customs trackers, buying agents, and miners all passed through the mazes of bridges and walkways of the hub. Thumping her tail again, Agnoix waved away Cassidy's questioning look.

If I'd been thinking, we might have been able to sneak onto a work cart and slip into the hub unnoticed. Too late for that now, she thought as they walked up to the inspection station. Two members of Xik'en security watched them, with their pointy teeth bared in agitation.

"Not more Sastreni revelers... haven't we had our

share tonight?" a female Xik'en said to the other, a smaller male.

"At least we haven't had the night Krozlan has. Those kids and their wild stories of murderous mammals has gotten too many spooked tonight," the smaller male said to his partner.

"You're right there Qhoxen." The female turned to Agnoix and Cassidy. "Now what are you kids doing here at the hub? You know you're not supposed to be down here without an escort."

"Nuzon, it's me, Agnoix," Agnoix said as she slid her abused Sastreni mask onto her head, exposing her face.

The puzzlement on the security guard's face turned to recognition. "Agnoix? Orlol's daughter, right? The one who wants to be an explorer instead of a dutiful Xik'en citizen." Her words were more playful than hurtful.

"That's right. I promised my Mom that we would come visit her and show her our Sastreni costumes. Oh, Nuzon. This is Caskad, a friend and newcomer to the station, so we're spending Sastreni together."

"Agnoix, you know the rules. We allow no unescorted youths in the mining hub, there's too much traffic and machinery in use, you could get hurt," Nuzon said, planting her taloned hands on her wide hips and blocking the way.

"Please, Nuzon!" Agnoix whined. "She knows we're coming and will meet us in the break room in the processing area. This is her only chance to see our costumes. She's working extra hours and my father is away. You know me, we'll be in and out quick, no one but us will know."

"Well," Nuzon said. She looked at her partner.

"They didn't sneak past, or pull any Sastreni pranks," Qhoxen said, his interest more focused on what was going on inside the hub than outside it. "I say let them go. You're only a kid once."

"Hmmm..." Nuzon replied. Eventually she nodded. "Okay, just this once, because it's Sastreni. There, wear these visitors' badges," Nuzon stuck two blue tags on the front of Agnoix's and Cassidy's costumes. "And stay on the blue path until you get to processing. You know the way, right? Agnoix, you won't stray? I'm putting my trust in you two."

"I know where we're going, Nuzon," Agnoix said. "Thank you for this, it... it means a lot."

As Agnoix and Cassidy passed by the security station, following the blue line on the floor, Nuzon shook her head. "Kids these days."

"I know what you mean," replied Qhoxen. "And what was up with their costumes? I didn't recognize either of them. In my day we dressed up as Tox'eix or another of the founders of our Empire like a good Xik'en. They waste youth on the young."

CHAPTER ELEVEN

The floor was a maze of colours as Agnoix and Cassidy followed the blue line through the open walkways of the processing hub. Fresh colours got added as routes branched, and they left behind some colours as the two walked along.

I hope Agnoix is paying better attention to where we're going than I am. I just can't believe how massive this place is, Cassidy thought to herself as she struggled to peer through the jaggedly cut eye holes of her costume at her surroundings.

As far as Cassidy could tell, she and Agnoix were in the middle of a vast cylinder that was criss-crossed with walkways, equipment elevators, and twisting cart ramps. A quick glance over a low railing showed that she and Agnoix were coming into the cylinder some place in its middle, since neither a floor nor ceiling were in view.

When no one was close to the pair, Cassidy leaned close to Agnoix and said: "How big is this station? It seems to go on forever."

Agnoix stopped at the junction point as a cart filled with Xik'ens dressed in harnesses and sporting purple badges passed by. She thought before she replied. "I don't know how to explain it in terms you would understand. Only that this mining complex began inside the largest asteroid in the belt and has grown through the generations, with other asteroids connected like a spoked wheel. This hub is the void left by the original asteroid."

Once the cart with harnessed Xik'ens passed, Agnoix looked around and stepped off the blue line they had been following and onto the purple.

"We need to hurry, Cassidy. We won't be able to talk our way out of the miner's area if we're caught; we will have to rely on your human luck."

"My dear Agnoix," Cassidy replied, her smile unseen by her friend. "Luck is how I live every day."

With the cart carrying the harnessed Xik'ens ahead of them, Agnoix and Cassidy crouched down and hurried to keep them in sight. As the cart left the open air hub and entered a tunnel opening with a purple display written above the hole, the women hurried after it.

Reminds me of Assyrian. I would love a direct word to word translation, Cassidy thought to herself.

They went as quietly as they could, though any noise they made was drowned by the echoing thunder that was being created in the hub.

Agnoix stopped and stared up at the purple display. "That means a group of miners are getting ready to fly out into the asteroid belt. They were the ones in the cart wearing harnesses." Pausing, Agnoix looked back at Cassidy and the spiraling walkways and bridges with people and equipment moving, and found herself rooted in place.

"Agnoix, what's wrong? I thought you said that this was the only way you could think of to get back outside."

"It is Cassidy, but... but I've never been in there, nor know what to expect. We've come to the end of my knowledge and I fear it won't be enough," Agnoix said. The distress in her voice was clear even through the Branch of Languages.

You should be ashamed, Cassidy. You should have guessed what kind of strain you were pulling on the poor kid. You were always so focused that you failed to see the plain and simple, Cassidy chided herself.

Cassidy placed her hand on the younger woman's shoulder. "I can take it from here, Agnoix, you have done way more than I could have ever expected. You saved my life at least twice and we've only known each other for less than a day. You head back home. With a bit of luck, your brother will be in enough trouble that they will ignore anything he says about me. I'm sorry that I have gotten you into trouble and didn't source any of the ARC crystals for the doctor, but just getting home will be challenge enough." She held out her hand. "We part ways here, friend Agnoix. I owe you more than I could say and I wish we could spend more time together. There is so much I could learn about your people, and share my world with you, but we must each go back to our own worlds and lives."

When Agnoix didn't take Cassidy's hand, Cassidy pushed forward and gave the young Xik'en woman a fierce hug, before dashing back into the tunnel towards her way home.

***

Turning away from Agnoix, who hadn't moved an

inch nor said a word, Cassidy pushed aside the emotions turning in her and got to work.

Okay, smarty pants: you left your guide behind and you're on your own. What are you going to do? Cassidy asked herself as she jogged down the winding tunnel, the fake tail in her costume banging against the wall as she moved.

"That's a good question," Cassidy muttered to herself, then froze in place as she came across the cart which had been transporting the Xik'ens that Agnoix identified as miners.

Cassidy leaned in and checked it out.

Other than the Xik'en equivalent of a fire extinguisher, a forgotten lunchbox, and the weirdly designed seats that took into account the Xik'en tail, Cassidy saw nothing of interest.

As she continued down the tunnel, Xik'en voices, too faint for the Branch of Languages to translate, issued from a narrow opening that branched off from the main tunnel.

Let's hope that two plus two makes four in this situation and those are my missing miners. Let's hope that is the tunnel to the flight deck or whatever they call it here.

Making sure that no one was nearby, Cassidy stepped into the tunnel, then stopped and looked back at the cart.

She cursed, then hurried back to the cart and picked up what she hoped was a fire extinguisher, holding it in both her hands. "I hope I don't have to injure anyone, but it doesn't hurt to be prepared." As she held her makeshift weapon at the ready, she once again followed the voices.

Whether it was the removing of the fire extinguisher from the cart or some other automated signal, the cart started to hum, and it drove on its own back the way it came.

"Probably pre-programmed. At least I hope so," Cassidy said, as the cart disappeared from view.

The tunnel wound around to a large open pit with a ramp leading down. Edging closer, Cassidy saw that the Xik'en miners were in a locker room and were suiting up in the same spacesuits and harnesses she had seen them with before.

Retreating from the edge of the pit, on the chance that one of them might look up, Cassidy retreated to the gallery window. Overlooking the locker pit, she got her first view of the mining bay.

"Holy scale rot," she said, her mouth open with shock.

CHAPTER TWELVE

"Goodbye Cassidy," Agnoix whispered to herself; the human woman having left her alone.

Goodbye to the first genuine friend you've ever had. Goodbye to your one and only chance to break the mold your family and culture are forcing you to fit within. Are you going to stand here and let it happen?

Scared and frustrated, Agnoix slammed her taloned fist against her thigh, the dull throbbing pain allowing a moment of clarity.

You've always idolized Brauxel, Warden of the Two Divines. Defender to all, whether they were outcast and refugee, and if Cassidy doesn't fit that then who would? So why did you wimp out? You're no hatchling that needs an adult to hold her hand. You're almost of age yourself, a grown Xik'en woman able to make her own decisions, so what do you decide? Are you going to let your friend walk into danger on her own, or are you going to defend her?

Slamming her fist against her thigh again, this time cracking her much abused homemade armour, Agnoix exclaimed: "I will defend my friend!"

She hurried after Cassidy, hoping to catch her before

anything bad happened.

The tunnel, with its purple lines on the floor, led off into several branches. But a quick look at the narrow script at the top of each door told her that what she wanted was further on, if for no other reason than the transport cart couldn't have travelled into those smaller corridors.

Maybe thinking about the cart isn't such a wonderful idea, she thought, for as soon as she did she heard the hum of its motor. It was getting closer -- FAST!

"Scale rot," Agnoix cursed, dashing into the nearest branching tunnel without time to see where it went.

Hurrying down the tunnel, Agnoix found herself in some kind of leisure room. Stools lined the walls, along with dust-covered work clothes and safety gear, and the sharp smell of fungal tea filled the air.

Emergency protocols pinned to the walls were covered in hand-written scribbles, along with a calendar featuring pictures of mining tools supplied by a well-known contractor. Then it dawned on her.

She was in the break room for those who did the rough job of sorting the asteroids before going into processing, those called 'Breakers'.

Agnoix knew little of these kinds of workers. The biggest and dumbest members of her society did this rough and dangerous work. At least, that was what her mother had always said, and had forbidden her to associate with the children of the Breakers. But as she had no friends regardless of social status, it hadn't mattered much to her.

Seeing an opportunity to find herself not in her colourful Sastreni costume, Agnoix acted.

Finding a pair of the thick, rough coveralls in her size

was her first problem, and where to change into them was her second. Shaking her head at the time she was wasting, Agnoix stripped off her costume. Heedless of the damage she was doing, the tortured and repaired fabric gave up the fight and she destroyed the costume of Brauxel without a second thought.

In place of the yellow and blue striped armour that signified the dual nature of Brauxel's commitment as a defender, was a new hero. Now stood young Agnoix in a patched and dust-covered pair of coveralls, with a helmet and face shield.

I should blend right in, Agnoix thought. As voices came up from behind her from the lavatory, her confidence evaporated and she made for the hatch at the other end of the break room.

Just as the shadows on the walls resolved into adult Xik'en, Agnoix passed through the hatch and into chaos.

***

"It's massive," Cassidy whispered as she looked down into the mining bay. She wasn't sure what she had been expecting. Asteroid mining wasn't really something she'd even given a second's thought about, but if she had, she doubted it would have looked like this.

It was shaped like a tiered valley, not unlike the Sacred Terraces in Peru, Cassidy reflected. Metal mining pods that resembled giant spiders filled the mining bay.

They were hauling chunks of sliced asteroid and dropping them into the centre of the valley, and the churning teeth within.

"It's massive," Cassidy repeated, as she tried to get

some sense of the scale. Her best guess would have been that it was several times larger than the largest airport she had even been in. "I was wrong, there's more than just that large grinder, each level has its own. I wonder if it's for processing different metals."

The voices in the locker pit below her changed in tone and Cassidy's musing cut itself off. Feet stomped, buckles snapped, and she heard a hatch open. With it, the smell of mineral dust flowed into the locker pit and up into the exhaust grill above Cassidy's head, threatening to make her sneeze.

In seconds, she saw the miners striding out to the top tier of the asteroid processing bay. They were walking to a group of eight mining spiders that had crew fueling and working on them, if her experience on Earth was any guide.

Must be shift change, as Agnoix said, Cassidy thought and felt a sense of shame. *I used that poor kid for my own ends and likely have gotten her into trouble, and I don't see any way to make it better than to leave. Gamgee will just have to do without his precious ARC crystals. It will be a miracle if I even get home.*

Breathing deeply, Cassidy looked down at the mining pods that were being made ready for flight, and she acted. Trusting that no one was below, she ran down the ramp, into the changing area and looked around. Several tunnels branched off. If she guessed by the smells, at least one was a bathroom, though she wasn't keen on putting her theory to the test. Along the walls were recessed lockers, with tags above each, which common sense would suggest were names. Clothes filled several of the lockers, while others were empty, and three contained spacesuits. The suits were of the same design that the miners who just left had been wearing.

Luckily enough, the first one she grabbed was close enough to her size that it didn't matter, though at this point she couldn't have afforded to be picky. Ripping off the costume that Agnoix had made for her, Cassidy was once again clothed as she had been when she'd abandoned her plane after coming through the portal.

"I need a long shower when I get home," she muttered as she got a whiff of herself, her nose crinkling.

Taking off the parachute and the homing device strapped to her left wrist, Cassidy felt a weight slide off her shoulders. The faint red flashing light confirmed that the beacon on board her plane was still active.

"That means I can find the way home, with a little luck. Okay, maybe more than a little."

Climbing into the Xik'en spacesuit wasn't the easiest thing to do on one's own, Cassidy found as she put one leg into the tail hole. But after some struggling she sealed it up, refastened the parachute over the suit, and strapped the homing device over the suit's wrist.

"It isn't fashionable, but it should do," Cassidy said as she looked at herself in a mirror.

Trusting that she had gotten the suit sealed, Cassidy picked up the awkward helmet and connected it to the neck ring. There was a hiss as the hot, muggy air filled her nostrils, telling her she had a good seal, even as the smell reminded her of a compost pile.

The view through the helmet was awkward for someone without the snout of a Xik'en. Cassidy managed well

enough to walk over to the hatch, the sad empty tail portion of her suit dragging along the floor.

With gloves that felt more akin to oven mitts, she hit
the yellow button beside the hatch, opening it. The vibration of its opening travelled up her body.

Feeling only a fraction of the confidence that she hoped
her bearing was showing the world, Cassidy walked into
the Xik'en filled mining bay.

CHAPTER THIRTEEN

Agnoix found herself in a press of bodies also suited like her, all bumping and jostling each other. Like a twig caught by a raging river, the young Xik'en found herself caught up in it.

Her panic was building the more the press of bodies tossed her around. There was the overwhelming smell of rock dust that even the best air filters couldn't extract. A tiny part of her mind remembered the words Cassidy had said: *Act like you own the world and people won't question you.*

Clenching her taloned fists, her lip curling until it exposed her needle-sharp teeth, Agnoix stopped fighting against the flow and hurried to run with it. Her yells of "Let me through; out of my way!" mingled with the other shouts and yells from her fellow Xik'en as they neared their destination.

Unseen hands thrust an air tank into her hands as she moved along. Agnoix watched the woman beside her clip it to her belt and connect it to her face shield, creating an airtight seal. The other Xik'en turned her head to regard Agnoix, her expression confused. Agnoix slid between bodies and out of the woman's view. Watching the others, she connected her own air tank and saw a tiny yellow bar light up on the side of the tank, showing it to be full.

The push of bodies formed a bottleneck at a hatch just ahead. Two blue suited Xik'en checked each miner in a procedure they had done countless times before, letting them into the mining bay.

Agnoix stopped breathing as one of the two blue suited Xik'en ran his talons over her suit, checking the air tank and helmet connection. "Nod if you can hear me," crackled over her helmet's speakers and, without thinking, Agnoix nodded. "Good, pass through." And in such an unceremonious manner, they thrust Agnoix into the massive mining bay that had given her race all the advantages it had.

Two steps into the mining bay, Agnoix stopped walking just to stop and stare. While she had lived here her whole life, like most people she had never been in the mining bay that had brought her society the wealth and privilege that it enjoyed. Sure, she had been in some processing departments, such as the ones where her mother worked, but that was cleaner, more civilized work, using a low gravity furnace to smelt base metal from stone into wire or ingots. Agnoix remembered a school trip in which they had refined the radioactive minerals and bars of gold, the products of each made faster than she could track them, but this was something else. Her people looked like ants as hundreds of them worked at different tiers. They supervised the crude crushing of the raw asteroids into their base parts and ejected the stone waste back out into space.

It was one of the most dangerous jobs on board the station, except for the actual mining and transport of the asteroids. Only the toughest -- or the most desperate -- took a job in primary processing, at a risk of life and limb just too great for most Xik'en.

Bumped from behind, Agnoix stopped her musings as the press of bodies heading to their assigned tier nearly ran her over. Shift results determined how much the workers earned, so more than a few eyes fell on the unmoving Agnoix.

Remember why you're here. Cassidy is likely close by, and while I've only known her a brief time, I'm sure she has everything well in hand.

Agnoix fell into step with a smaller group of suited Xik'en, who made their way up the winding ramps to the top of the grinding tiers. She couldn't help but wonder if the stone she saw, being moved in skids driven by suited Xik'en, would end up in her mother's processing area tonight. *I know so little of what happens here; I was eager to explore and see unknown worlds. Maybe looking at ourselves should be part of my exploration too.* Agnoix struggled up the winding ramp. The long night, with no food and the extra weight of suit and tank, began to sap her energy. She reached the top tier before she collapsed, her legs wobbling from exhaustion.

People, mining pods, and hoists crowded the flight deck, moving the fresh rocks into the many tiers below them. So very far below, Agnoix realized, as the extreme height made her dizzy and forced her to refocus on her level.

Unlike the other grinding tiers devoted to metals and

minerals, Agnoix had come to where the Vao stones went through their pre-processing.

The group of nine suited Xik'en took up their stations on a conveyor belt and, with hand-held lasers, began cutting the hunks of the rare crystal from the surrounding stone.

Agnoix watched as one large male Xik'en gripped a hunk of grey asteroid half as big as Agnoix. Standing it on its end and balancing it one-handed, he used a hand-held laser to slice out three pieces of green Vao stone. They were each as big as her hand, and he dropped them onto the conveyor that led into the wall for more refining. The major pieces of the valuable stone harvested, the worker pushed the rest of the rock into the grinder. They would harvest any smaller pieces and use them in smaller pieces of technology, like Agnoix's Branch of Languages that Cassidy was wearing.

His task done, the large Xik'en stretched and was about to reach for another hunk of asteroid when he spied Agnoix. She was standing at the end of his workstation, staring at the nine workers, her tail twitching in nervousness.

Without thinking, Agnoix waved. "Continue on, just on my inspection tour," she said, picking up a handful of the rare Vao stones and turning them, pretending to examine them. She left the male Xik'en confused.

She jumped when alarms sounded, and panic spread through the flight deck above.

And here I was concerned that I wouldn't be able to find Cassidy, Agnoix though, making a dash for the last ramp leading to the flight deck, Vao stones in hand.

***

The inside of the mining bay was a maze of activity, with people and equipment going in every direction. Mechanical arms grabbed the massive hunks of asteroid when the mining pods dropped them after they came 'inside.' Slowing her steps to get a better look, what Cassidy took as random movements by the pods, rocks, and arms was in fact choreographed. It made her think of dancers in a massive stage production. The flying dust and constant rumbling of the grinders that sent vibrations were special effects. The entire atmosphere put her in the mind of a Shakespearean tragedy, and she half expected to see three hags materialize off to one side.

Realizing that the distance between herself and the Xik'en pilots she was following was getting larger, Cassidy picked up speed. She fought the urge to grab the empty tail of the spacesuit to make walking easier, and focused on what was in front of her.

From what Cassidy could tell, there was an invisible barrier at least four times the size of an Olympic swimming pool in front of her. Each mining pod passed through the barrier to reach the pressurized -- though dusty -- primary mining bay. The weight of open space and her recent brush with death at its hand gripped her chest with a fist of ice. Cassidy forced herself to continue walking toward the void of space as her instincts screamed at her to flee.

To distract herself from the approaching barrier between her and the void of space, Cassidy tried to follow the several conversations that were being broadcast through her spacesuit.

As far as she could tell, she was tuned into a passive channel. It seemed to only pick up those conversations happening within a five metre radius, but she didn't want to test that theory by speaking.

The first of the Xik'en mining pilots got to their craft and began an inspection of the space pod. Cassidy watched as best she could for any tips that would make this hare-brained idea of hers have a better chance of success than its current percent: zero. Once he was done, he watched as the rest of the crew did the same before waving them over to an empty spot in front of the line of mining pods.

Her radio crackled again, and this time it seemed that it was the first pilot speaking.

The Branch of Languages once again translated the Xik'en language, and Cassidy realized suddenly that she had no way to return it to the adolescent Xik'en girl.

Pushing her regret aside for a minute, Cassidy tried to focus on what the lead mining pilot was saying.

"... and you and Zausk take the targets in sector 42 Alpha. We have tagged those rocks for that order of copper wire on that fresh colony world we're putting a trading hub on. That leaves Sist and myself to cut and grab that rich vein of Vao stones the surveyors found last week. There should be three trips each if we can cut the raw rock small enough for easy transport. Sound good?"

As the other eight members of the Xik'en mining crew made various noises of agreement, Cassidy worked her way behind them. Heading for the lead ship, with its bubble hatch open and inviting, Cassidy started to get her hopes up.

Within metres of the ship, her radio crackled again.

"Hey you, what do you think you're doing at my pod?"

Fearing capture when freedom of a sort was within reach, Cassidy ran towards the mining pod, when disaster struck. With a swinging tail section and boots more akin to clown shoes than human-sized boots, Cassidy made it only three strides before the toe of her boot caught. She stumbled and could not recover. She went down in a heap, her helmet bouncing off the deck.

Shaken and holding an elbow numb with pain, Cassidy didn't pay any attention to the voices coming through her helmet speakers until she felt a heavy hand on her shoulder.

"Are you okay, citizen? Are you supposed to be here? That's my pod and..." The Xik'en miner broke off in mid-sentence as he rolled the injured human over and got a look at the face within the helmet.

For several moments the Xik'en pilot just stared, his reptilian face trying to puzzle out what he was seeing. As the reality of the situation dawned upon him, he let go of Cassidy. The Xik'en miner stood above her, looking at the space-suited mammal with a pack strapped to its chest and a red blinking light attached to its left wrist.

"Everyone get back! Flee!" he shouted over the radio, so loud that it threatened to deafen Cassidy. "It's a murderous mammal, and it's carrying a bomb! Terrorist! Flee!"

Taking his own advice, the Xik'en pilot pushed past his confused comrades. He knocked down the first one, which had the ripple effect of a piece of meat thrown into a pool of piranhas, as chaos broke loose.

Frantic and garbled radio transmissions spoke over each other, fanning the flames of fear and confusion into an inferno.

In seconds, the well-organized hive of industry that was a staple of the Xik'en mining bay became a riot.

Out of control mechanical arms, rock grinders spinning empty, and running mine workers were everywhere as confused reports spread through the massive bay.

Emergency lights flashed as equipment overheated and got overloaded with material with no one to remove it.

Sirens blared in various tones, which made Cassidy thankful that the helmet shielded her from the worst of them.

Countless Xik'en ran for the exits, though since dozens rushed within arms of her reach, they did not understand what they were running from.

One older female Xik'en reached down a taloned hand and hoisted Cassidy to her feet, shouting: "Get off the flight deck, miner. There's a rogue mammal here threatening to blow us all up!" With that, the good Samaritan mixed in with the flow of bodies, leaving Cassidy dazed and confused.

Forcing herself to move, Cassidy got herself under the hull of the mining pod that she had wanted to steal and placed a shaky hand on the open canopy. Pausing, Cassidy scanned the area, thinking she heard her name being called out.

She lifted the visor of her helmet, smoke and dust burning its way into her lungs. Over the din of a multitude of alarms, she heard her name called again.

"Cassidy Cane!"

Hordes of Xik'en were pushing and shoving their way to exit the vast mining bay. A few Xik'en tried to control and direct the flow of people, but their efforts were in vain. Cassidy saw that several clumps of Xik'en mine workers had turned the chaos into something more serious, and punches were being thrown.

Again Cassidy heard her name.

Out of the chaos of shoving bodies, a smaller than normal Xik'en pushed her way through the reptilian wall, and Cassidy could see it was Agnoix.

"Here Agnoix!" Cassidy yelled, and began waving her arms. She smashed her wrist against the side of the mining pod and stopped, but it had been enough motion for the youthful Xik'en girl to notice, and she changed direction to connect with Cassidy.

The joy of seeing a familiar and friendly face rushed through Cassidy and lifted the weight from her chest that adrenaline had been keeping aside.

Truth be known, Cassidy hadn't been very confident that she would have been able to fly the mining pod without some basic instructions. If the confusion held for a couple more minutes, Cassidy could get a crash course in written Xik'en. But before that, she moved out from under the mining pod and swallowed Agnoix in a big, clumsy hug, causing the young Xik'en to drop what she was carrying.

From her hands fell five pieces of Vao stones the size of an enormous egg, still embedded in asteroid stones. They tumbled and fell to the mining bay floor.

"I grabbed these for you, Cassidy. I thought, you

know, our deal? That you'd take me as far as this portal so I can see your world?" Agnoix said between gasping breaths.

Cassidy stared down at the Vao stones that had brought her to this strange place, and couldn't help but laugh all the harder now that they had fallen at her feet.

Squeezing Agnoix all the tighter until the younger woman hissed in discomfort, Cassidy said: "I think you've earned your glimpse of the portal that connects our two worlds, my friend." Releasing the young Xik'en, Cassidy waved her sore hand at the pod. "Plus, I could use a little help to figure out where the 'on switch' is with this thing."

"I'm sure between us, friend Cassidy, we can figure it out," Agnoix said, while thinking: *At least I hope we can. I may have slept through the classroom documentaries about mining now that I think about it...*

As the pair bent down to pick up the fallen Vao stones, Cassidy looked over Agnoix's shoulder and saw a small group of Xik'en off to one side. The speaker, as far as Cassidy could tell, was the same one who had discovered her. He was jumping up and down while pointing in their direction.

"Ah, Agnoix? I think it's time to leave, and I mean RIGHT NOW!" Grabbing the young Xik'en by the arm, Cassidy pulled her to her feet as the group of Xik'en ran towards them with make-shift weapons in their hands.

"Can I get a lift?" Cassidy asked, and gasped in surprise as Agnoix gripped her around the waist and hoisted her up into the bubble of the mining pod. *My goodness, these Xik'en are strong!* Cassidy thought to herself, even as she tried to make head and tails of the inside of the mining pod. She flinched when Agnoix pulled herself in like a gymnast. *Darn strong! I hope to never get on her nasty side.*

Standing on the bottom set of mechanical limbs of the mining pod, Cassidy looked over Agnoix's shoulder at the small group of angry Xik'en miners that were getting closer.

While Cassidy was no expert, their body language and the fact that they were holding make-shift weapons suggested to her that they didn't want to invite her to tea.

"I think NOW would be a marvellous time to get out of here, Agnoix," Cassidy said. "Do you think you could fly this thing?"

Agnoix looked over Cassidy's shoulder at the profusion of buttons and controllers that made her feel weak in the knees.

Perhaps Cassidy saw some dread pass through the young Xik'ens face, or could just sense it based on years of being exposed to different cultures.

"Now that's silly, Agnoix, we would need to switch places and we don't have time for that. I'm the pilot, you act as navigator, and my first command is that you get that hatch shut because our friends will be here any second."

Agnoix realized that Cassidy's suggestion was timely, and struggled to turn around in the cramped cockpit.

She turned, smacking Cassidy alongside her head with her tail just once, then hit the close button. The dome of the egg-shaped cockpit closed, and everything became quiet.

As Agnoix began the awkward process of trying to

turn around again, Cassidy asked: "Doesn't this thing have a seat or something? Do they fly standing up? This is the oddest setup I've ever seen."

Ha! This is something I can help with, Agnoix thought.

"We have little use for seats, Cassidy. Just lean into the centre groove. Your body shape being weird with those lumps and bumps will make it uncomfortable. Oh, and ignore the four hooks around the edges, those are for the harness so you don't get thrown around." Watching as Cassidy leaned into the body groove meant for a Xik'en, Agnoix almost jumped out of her scales as a bang rang in her ears. The mining pod vibrated. Putting out a hand to steady herself, she almost crushed Cassidy, who yelped in pain.

"Get out here, mammal. We'll show you what we do with your kind!" yelled a miner with a pry bar in his hand, having just smashed against the hatch not a hand's width from Agnoix's snout and about to swing again.

"I think we should leave now, Cassidy!" Agnoix said, turning away from the angry Xik'en.

"I'd love too, but I don't read Xik'en and I need your help, remember?" Cassidy said, her cheeks flushed.

"Oh, sorry." Agnoix jumped again as the pry bar smashed against the clear hatch.

I know they make the glass to withstand the abuse out in outer space; I hope it can survive a few more minutes.

"Agnoix, I need you now!" Cassidy yelled.

Smash!

"Sorry! Okay, there are two handles, one's up and to the side, the other is down to the other side. I'm sorry, I don't remember which is which, this looks so different from the videos I've seen."

"That's fine, Agnoix, I'll figure it out. But I need to know how to start the engine or whatever this thing uses to move," Cassidy shouted, just as several more bangs shook the mining pod as more mining bay personal directed their fear towards Cassidy and Agnoix. "Now would be good, Agnoix."

Leaning over her friend, Agnoix reached out her taloned left hand and smashed down on the yellow power button. That activated the thrusters and the whole mining pod vibrated as if it were an idling train on its tracks.

"Well, I have a 50/50 chance of getting this right," Cassidy said as she jerked the handle in her right hand back. The mining pod shot to the left and smashed into the mining bay wall, scattering the group of angry miners, tails and talons hurrying away.

"Okay, let's try this again." Cassidy eased the left handle backwards, and the pod went to the right until it was floating high above the largest set of cylindrical grinders in the whole mining bay. Each the size of a train car, Cassidy would have hated to think what they could have done to their stolen mining pod. Peering forward and looking down at the massive grinders that could swallow the mining pod in a second, Cassidy took a death breath.

"Let's see, if right back is left, and left back is right, what are the chances that left forward is up and right forward is down?" Cassidy said, looking over her shoulder at her friend crouched behind her. Agnoix's reptilian eyes were wide. "You know, they wired your brains kinda different. Has anyone ever told you Xik'ens that?"

Looking out the left side of the cockpit, Cassidy saw

that the miners who had attacked them were now running for their own mining pods. Pods that they would have had years of skill and experience to master against her crash course.

"Dang. Okay, Agnoix, I think I might have a handle on this. Now how do we go forward or reverse?"

"You grab this toggle with your tail and..." Agnoix's voice trailed off.

"Are you kidding me?" Cassidy yelled as she watched the first asteroid miner pop the hatch on one of the mining pods.

"I can do it, I know I can, Cassidy. Just trust me," Agnoix said as she stuck her tail into the shallow socket in the floor and gripped the toggle. With the finite control common with her race, the young Xik'en had forward and backward sorted out in seconds.

"Expert job, Agnoix," Cassidy said. "And now for the elephant in the room, how do you get out of here?" She thrust her chin at the apartment building-sized hole in the wall, with nothing between them but the naked void of space. "I've been trying my very best NOT to even look at it, but the time has come. Please tell me you know how to get through that, Agnoix."

I must show no sign of doubt. Cassidy is counting on me and she's afraid; this must be so foreign to her.

"That's easy, Cassidy," Agnoix said. "Just fly through it. They fit the pod with a shield key allowing it and anything attached to it to fly through. Everything else bounces off."

At least I'm pretty sure that's how it works, and assuming the key was turned on when the pod powered up, and assuming the damage taken hasn't broken it.

"You sure?"

"I have no doubt, Cassidy," Agnoix lied to her friend.

The angry miners lifted off the flight deck and gave chase, the pilots able to use the mechanical arms fitted with grips, lasers, and drills. Cassidy and Agnoix aimed for the stars twinkling between the asteroids, with their stolen mining pod like a stumbling drunkard charging through.

CHAPTER FOURTEEN

Well, maybe 'charging' wasn't the right word for how Cassidy and Agnoix left the mining bay.

In a move that resembled what stunt drivers would call 'drifting' around the corners on a track, the mining pod breached the environmental seal at an oblique angle, and no faster than a walk.

"Agnoix, we will need some speed if we want to get away from those miners back there," Cassidy shouted over the gong that sounded as the pod passed through the meter-thick shielding separating the dusty, yet breathable, mining bay and the void of space.

"I might give you more speed if you would point this thing in the direction you want to go. I'm scared we'll crash if we go any faster," Agnoix replied, her own fear and frustration coming through.

"Sorry, Agnoix, it's this blasted helmet. It's too big and the view port is all wrong for someone without a snout. Help me get it off would you?"

Taking her hands off the controls, Cassidy struggled to get the helmet off while laying down. Once Agnoix got her talons involved with a quick twist and a pop, the helmet floated free.

"That's much better. Thanks, Agnoix," Cassidy said as she gripped the flight handles and pulled herself back down into place. "I see why the miners had those harnesses. Every time I use the controls my body wants to follow along. At least I'm getting a good core workout."

Confused by what Cassidy meant, Agnoix realized that understanding the words differed from understanding their meaning, but still got the bare bones of what Cassidy was talking about.

"Yes, the mining pods are much too small to carry gravity generators, and they would likely make it harder in the long run. I've heard that the best miners are also the best swimmers; able to work in three dimensions and all that."

"That makes sense," Cassidy said, looking over her shoulder at her friend and getting her first look of the mining station from the outside. Her mouth fell open.

While grad school had been a while ago for Cassidy, and chemistry had never been her strong point, some tiny part of her mind whispered to her. The Xik'en mining station resembled a tetrahedral molecule, with a centre hub -- from which they had just escaped -- and four arms jutting out from it so it looked like a caltrop. No matter what way you looked at it, one 'point' was up.

Agnoix had told Cassidy all this, but she had never really believed it until now. Asteroids the size of human cities connected by tubes so Xik'en could travel.

"I just can't get over this... this complex, Agnoix. Humanity has nothing the size or complexity of this. There must be room for thousands of people there," Cassidy said, her voice a whisper as she tried to drink in as many details as possible of the marvel.

"Tens of thousands actually, though about a third of the people are short-term visitors passing through. My people don't normally like to move around a lot, but other races come here since the station sees so much traffic."

At the word 'traffic,' Cassidy's mind realized that the mountains and hills that she saw on the various asteroids were in fact dozens of space ships, each docked on the outside of the asteroids.

"Why didn't I bring my sketchbook or a camera with me," Cassidy scolded herself, just as the collision happened.

In their combined nervousness and excitement, the two had forgotten what brought them to this point. The thud of another mining pod striking theirs and throwing them forward against the dash of the pod brought their situation back to the present.

The other mining pods' mechanical limbs reached out with grips, lasers, and drills, none of which would be good for the two of them. Cassidy and Agnoix fought to untangle their limbs from each other and resume their make-shift driving setup.

"Give me forward now, Agnoix," Cassidy yelled, twisting the controllers so that the little mining pod corkscrewed away from the station. "A little more speed Agnoix. I assume he's still back there?"

Focusing all her attention on trying to not crush her friend in the cramped cockpit AND apply the right amount of speed, Agnoix thought she was doing a magnificent job for this being her first time driving. That was until she looked behind her.

"Scale rot!" Agnoix cursed. "He has hold of one of our limbs with a gripper and is dragging himself closer. Cassidy, what do we do?"

"I'm thinking!" Cassidy yelled, refocusing her attention on the view outside and trying to ignore the braid that kept floating in front of her face. "Flying through the magnetic shield that protects the station is the same as that in the mining bay, right?" Cassidy asked, her tone back to normal. "I mean, I don't have to do anything? Just fly through?"

I don't think I'm ready to be an adult, if knowing all the answers to questions people ask will continue, Agnoix thought as she stared back at the mining pod that had them in its grip and saw that a spinning drill attached to yet another arm was seeking them.

"Yes, absolutely, as you said," Agnoix babbled. "Just hurry, Cassidy, he's got a drill."

"Fudge nuggets," Cassidy swore as she shifted course towards the nearest shield emitters.

With only the barest idea of how the hundreds of metal spheres that formed the bubble of protection around the mining complex worked, Cassidy decided that it was time to show the Xik'en miners a thing or two about driving earth-style.

Seeing the apartment building-sized metal sphere getting closer and closer, Agnoix felt a little queasy and slowed them down. "Ah, Cassidy, what are you doing? I don't like this plan..."

"I will teach our friend back there about a little game we play back home called 'chicken', so pour on the speed again. I know what I'm doing," Cassidy said, as she leaned deeper into the pilot's position.

Seeing the drill skip along the metal hide of their pod, and the lights of at least three more chasers, Agnoix made the quick decision to trust her warm-blooded friend. Using her prehensile tail, Agnoix threw their pod into motion and prayed to her ancestors she'd made the right choice.

The surge in speed caught Cassidy by surprise. She wasn't sure that Agnoix would risk herself and put her trust in a being that she'd been told her whole life was their equivalent of the bogeyman. And if she was being honest with herself, she wouldn't have been angry if Agnoix had refused to go on. It would likely have meant a quick walk out an airlock for Cassidy, but at least Agnoix would have been safe.

This isn't the time for What if's. You can shake this fool, and make it home. I'm sure they'll go easy on Agnoix, she's just a kid, and I'll make sure she tells them I forced her into helping me.

Pushing down her doubts and worries, Cassidy poured all her attention at the metal sphere growing in front of her.

At first Cassidy thought the gleaming sphere was the size of a cargo van, then an apartment building, and now realized that it was bigger than a cargo ship and filled their view.

How bloody big is this thing? Cassidy thought to herself, before calling over her shoulder: "Is our buddy still with us?"

"He's still there, and I can feel the drill against our hull," Agnoix said. "I'm getting scared, Cassidy."

"Me too kiddo, this should be over in just a minute." Cassidy did her best to comfort her young friend as she aimed their pod for one of the antenna, streaks of blue fire outlining it like a Christmas tree.

As the crackling energy reached out and struck their pod, the Xik'en miner decided that today wasn't his day to die. He pulled away in a hairpin turn, which broke off his drill, leaving it sticking out of their mining pod.

"He's gone!!! Cassidy, he left, turn, turn, TURN!!!" Agnoix shrieked, her fear allowing her to forget that she was in charge of their speed. Cassidy pulled their mining pod out of its suicidal run with a sharp twist of the controls. They passed by the menacing antenna without harm and breached the magnetic shielding around the mining station -- keeping it free from errant asteroids -- and made it to open space.

"Well, maybe not open space," Cassidy muttered as the wealth of the Xik'en was all around them; asteroids from the size of a chicken's egg to ones as big as an ocean liner, and their density increasing the farther in Cassidy could see.

"Ah Agnoix, maybe ease up on the speed? Things are kinda crowded in here."

"I don't think we should. There are three other pods behind us and they're getting closer," Agnoix replied.

"I just hate it when a date doesn't get the hint," Cassidy quipped. "Okay, I will see if I can lose them inside this shifting maze. You keep your hand, er... tail on the throttle, we might need to brake in a hurry."

Agnoix gripped her friend's shoulder and gave it a gentle squeeze of agreement, and the battered mining pod flew into the thickest part of the asteroid belt.

Later, when Cassidy thought back about that maddening flight within the Xik'en asteroid belt, she was only able to recall the barest of details. There were the near misses from asteroids that were almost invisible until they were right in front of them. The constant pursuit by the miners as they tried to flank them. The shouts of 'watch out, left, turn, and BRAKES!' that each of them yelled at the other, which echoed within in the small cockpit. Despite all that, it had still been good luck that saved them. Or rather, the bad luck of one miner chasing them.

"Something's happened, Cassidy," Agnoix shouted, easing up on their reckless speed. "One of the other pods either hit an asteroid or broke down. All I see is a trail of loose rock and venting atmosphere. The other two pods are moving to give it aid."

"I hope the miner is okay, but this is our chance for an escape. Give me some forward movement, okay, Agnoix?"

Looking back at the scene behind them, Agnoix hoped that the miner would get the attention he deserved.

He meant Cassidy harm, but I just can't wish him ill. He likely has a family waiting for him back home, Agnoix thought.

Home. A wave of homesickness rushed through Agnoix and the adventure of another world didn't hold the appeal it once did. Her previous plan of escaping to Cassidy's world no longer seemed like as much fun as before. Maybe there was a place for her in Xik'en society. Maybe not a traditional place, but a place nonetheless.

I just need to make sure Cassidy gets home okay first, then

I'll have time to think.

"Agnoix?"

"Sorry Cassidy, I was just making sure the miner is okay. It looks like the other two are grabbing his pod and are towing it back towards the station." Using her tail on the controller, Agnoix started the pod forward again with Cassidy at the controls.

CHAPTER FIFTEEN

"There, I'm sure of it. The plane must be close, the flashes ARE getting faster," Cassidy said as she tapped the blinking red light strapped to her left wrist.

The hunt for Cassidy's plane had taken much longer than either of them had expected. Their flight from the miners was more important than noting their direction. With only the barest understanding of the secondary controls, they'd had a lot of backtracking to do to make their way back to the edge of the asteroid field.

Agnoix thought about mentioning how low they were getting on fuel, but since Cassidy wasn't aware, the young Xik'en didn't see the need to worry her friend.

"I agree Cassidy, the blinks are getting faster, but they have been for a while and I don't see this 'airplane' of yours floating around anywhere," Agnoix said. The lack of food, water and sleep had caught up with them both.

"Me either, but it must be around here someplace..." Cassidy said, scanning the crowded space around them through the cockpit window. "THERE! Down on that asteroid. The microgravity of that rock must have pulled it in."

Laying upside down with its missing canopy gone, Gamgee's experimental plane was a sight for sore eyes, even with a crushed wing and a buckled frame.

"It doesn't look like it will ever fly again. Not that I thought I would get that lucky. But since the homing beacon is still receiving, that means there's power, and that means the portal detector is likely okay. Gamgee reinforced it." Staring down at the only piece of familiar tech she'd seen since she flew into this dimension hit Cassidy hard. She hoped that Agnoix didn't see the moisture in her eyes.

"Okay, the easiest and safest way for me to get the portal beacon out of the plane is to figure out how these mechanical arms work. That's assuming they still work after the abuse they've been through," Cassidy said.

I've never been planet-side, but even if I was I doubt I would fly in anything so rudimentary. These humans do surprising things with few resources. I wonder if we Xik'en could learn a lesson or two from them, Agnoix mused as she looked at the craft which had brought her friend to this dimension.

"I think I can help with that, Cassidy," Agnoix said. "I may not feel up to the stunt flying that you seem to enjoy, but this thing," she pointed at the mechanical arms hanging on the outside of the pod like forgotten toys in a playground, "I have experience with stuff like this. It's not much different from the bubble gun I used to save you."

Cassidy only had the haziest idea how the emergency life saving equipment the Xik'en had created worked, and felt relief for the offer of help.

Good on you, Agnoix. I wonder if you would have been this forthcoming before we'd met. I get the impression you've grown a lot in such a brief span of time, Cassidy thought to herself, and chose not to give voice to her thoughts for fear of embarrassing Agnoix. "Sounds like a splendid plan. Let's get close, then you can take over and show me how it's done."

In a series of short controlled bursts, Cassidy and Agnoix got their stolen mining pod to within a few meters of Gamgee's experimental plane.

"Okay, your turn Agnoix," Cassidy said, and the two women switched places in the cramped confines of the cockpit. "I wonder how those circus clowns manage it?"

She received a confused look from Agnoix.

"Ah... never mind, it would take too much time to explain and it isn't that funny."

Once a Xik'en shaped body was laying in the body groove of the mining pod, the pair had much more room than before. Cassidy took the time for a good stretch to loosen her sore muscles before leaning over her friend's shoulder.

"Okay, Agnoix, show me how it's done." Cassidy patted her friend's shoulder before pointing. "I'd suggest using two grippers on the pontoon and rolling the plane towards us, being mindful of the wings." Seeing that her Earth-based words were giving the Branch of Languages a hard time, Cassidy used simpler language. "See the two long tubular things? Those are pontoons, they allow the plane to float atop of water."

"I thought you said this machine flew way up in the sky?" Agnoix interrupted.

"It does, ah... it can do both. I'll explain later, if there's time," Cassidy said, trying to get them back on track. "Just grab one of the long tubes and lift the plane off the aster-oid. We need to access the side against the rock."

Cassidy watched as Agnoix used the hand controllers to grip the bottom of the plane with the long mechanical limbs.

Once it was rolled towards the cockpit of the pod, Cassidy saw that any thought of taking the plane back through the portal would be a waste of time.

"Part of me hoped that I'd be able to use the plane as a glider and slip back through the portal into Earth's atmosphere. But that," she pointed at the crumpled tail fins, "means that plan is out. I must risk the parachute and hope the rescue boat is still nearby."

Seeing that she was upsetting Agnoix, Cassidy forced a smile. "It was wishful thinking. I'll be fine, I promise. The rescue boat had orders to stay in the area for a week; I'm sure it will all work out. I do crazy stuff like this all the time."

Brilliant job, Cassidy, dump more worry on the girl, Cassidy scolded herself, then set to distracting Agnoix.

"Okay, back to the job at hand, my friend. You see the empty cockpit? Not that dissimilar to this one, though we humans like to sit on our butts more than you Xik'ens do." Cassidy attempted to lighten the mood, and Agnoix rewarded her with a slight smile, her needle-sharp teeth shining in the cabin light. "In the front cockpit, you see that small square box bolted to the dash, right?" When Agnoix nodded, Cassidy continued. "I need to see the screen on the front of it. Do you feel up to playing with a laser?"

The prospect of using the laser distracted Agnoix from

her worries, and she set herself to work.

She just needs a little self-confidence. I wasn't any different at her age, Cassidy thought.

Cassidy smiled as she watched Agnoix bring the robotic arm with the asteroid cutting laser on its tip up against the clasp holding the portal detector in place.

She's finding her own way and is stronger than she might think and just needs a little self confidence.

"Okay Cassidy, I think I have it lined up, through I can't be sure."

"I'm sure you have it bang on. Ah... you know I need the detector in one piece right?" Cassidy said, her tone soft.

"I understand. And if I'm understanding this laser right, I have it on the lowest setting and will just give it a quick burst."

"Then I say fire away, Captain Agnoix!"

Shaking her head at her weird human friend, Agnoix double checked her settings on the laser and tapped the thumb toggle.

One side of the metal band holding the portal detector glowed orange and popped away.

"Wow, I saw nothing, Agnoix."

"You can't see lasers in a vacuum, Cassidy."

"Ah yes... I probably learned that once, but that knowledge got pushed out by something else later."

"And you say Xik'en brains are wired weird..." Agnoix mumbled as she reset the mining laser. Within minutes, the portal detector was safely in the mechanical hands of the mining pod.

"It seems a little... ah, basic, Cassidy. Is all your world's technology like this?" Agnoix asked, unable to help herself as they looked at the blinking green arrow on the screen of the portal detector.

Cassidy chuckled. "No, not all. Gamgee knows that sometimes my adventures can be hard on gear, so he likes to make things simple. He believes that boys are smarter than girls and I don't correct him. I won't want to see him cry." Cassidy winked.

I will miss you Cassidy, I wish we could have had more time together, Agnoix thought, not trusting her voice to speak.

"Okay then, the portal is nearby. We should hurry; I assume your mother is looking for you. I'm sorry if I got you in trouble Agnoix. I have this habit of getting myself into trouble and dragging others along whether they want to go or not."

"Don't be foolish! It was my decision to rescue you and try to find a way off the mining complex. If I get into trouble because I helped a mammal, seeing the look on Axaik's face was worth it!"

Laughing, they hugged, and the laughter evaporated into sad looks as they made their way to the portal, each lost in their own thoughts.

"I can barely see it," Agnoix said as she leaned over Cassidy's shoulder. "If it wasn't for the glittering of the narrow funnel of rock dust around it, I would never have seen it."

"And that's likely why none of your people have come to my dimension," Cassidy replied, staring at the portal and her way home.

"Here, don't forget these," Agnoix said, handing Cassidy the five rough Vao stones that she'd stolen while in the mining bay.

"Why is it woman's clothing never has pockets?" Cassidy muttered to herself, as she tried to figure out a way to carry the stones. With an "Ah ha!" she pulled down the pilot suit far enough to stuff the stones into the empty tail section of her Xik'en spacesuit.

"I don't make a very good Xik'en, do I?" Cassidy asked with a grin.

"Maybe not, but you're a wonderful friend. I will miss you Cassidy." Agnoix's upper lip was quivering, exposing her needle-sharp teeth.

"I will miss you too. I won't make you any promises, but I may be back, and if I am, I'll be better prepared. Thank you for seeing me as more than a 'warm-blood'. Few of my people would accept the call to help an alien stranger."

They both paused and just stared at each other, neither wanting the parting to happen but knowing that it must.

"You're sure your mask and tank from the mining bay will let you breathe? I don't want to risk your life trying to get home," Cassidy asked, pointing to the equipment Agnoix took from the mining bay when she disguised herself as a worker.

"I'm sure, Cassidy. The masks and tanks are for more than the dust in the mining bay. They're there in case of a failure of the barrier shield. My people are pragmatic if nothing else. I'll be fine, trust me." The suppressed fear in the adolescent Xik'en voice was easy to hear, but Cassidy pretended not to.

"And you can pilot this home? Do you want me to go through it again?" Cassidy asked, leaning down towards the controls.

"Stop, Cassidy, I'll be fine, you showed me what to do, and I watched as you flew. I'm sure I can get back to the mining station with no problems. I promise to go slow and steady like you said," Agnoix repeated. They had already gone over all this once before, but now that the portal was right there and Cassidy's leaving had become real, they were both drawing it out.

"Here," Cassidy said, and reached up to remove the Branch of Languages that had been allowing the two to communicate.

"Wait, Cassidy," Agnoix said, holding her hands up. "You keep it. Maybe this doctor of yours can make use of it and make more. Consider it a gift."

Cassidy's hand paused as she considered, then gave her head a slight shake. "No, it's yours and it's too precious a gift to give away. Plus, if you're questioned when you get home you can say that you couldn't understand me, since no filthy mammal would give up such a beautiful piece."

It had taken some back and forth, but Cassidy and Agnoix agreed that Agnoix should tell a version of the truth, because as Cassidy put it: "The best lies are two-thirds truth." Agnoix was to admit to firing the bubble gun that saved her life, as any good Xik'en would do. It was not her fault that the life she saved was a warm-blood. It had been impossible to tell. Then she was to say that Cassidy had taken her hostage. As a helpless victim of a dangerous mammal, Agnoix had been dragged through the mining station, from which Cassidy had stolen a shuttle, and they had both escaped.

And when the 'noble and brave' Xik'en miners could not stop Cassidy and rescue the helpless Agnoix, she had

had to rescue herself.

Cassidy took them to the primitive craft and attempted to recover it using the mining pod. When she was distracted, Agnoix had opened the mining pod's hatch and blasted Cassidy out into the void of space.

While there were a couple holes in the story, the biggest one to Agnoix's mind was that Axaik and his drunken friends had seen Agnoix trying to hide and protect Cassidy. Still, she decided not to burden Cassidy with that concern.

Before Agnoix could object again, Cassidy peeled off the Branch of Languages.

The slight warmth and tingle she had felt while wearing the alien translation device faded, and with it, her ability to communicate to her friend.

"I know you can't understand me, Agnoix. I'll be forever thankful for you saving my life and showing a stranger your kindness. You've given me a lot to think about," Cassidy said. She placed the Branch of Languages in her friend's hand, closing Agnoix's talons around it.

Smiling, Cassidy picked up the discarded mining pilot helmet and struggled to put it on. Agnoix shoved the Branch of Languages into the pocket of her miner's suit and helped Cassidy connect the helmet, insuring that the air was flowing.

Once Agnoix had her own breathing mask on, they double checked each other's breathing equipment twice. Cassidy gave a double thumbs-up and Agnoix hit the hatch door and heard the pumps reclaim what air there was within the cockpit before opening the door.

The cold of the void flowed into the cockpit of the tiny mining pod. Agnoix could see the moisture that had been gathering on the inside of the windows. Unable to handle the hot breath of a mammal, it flash-froze into a beautiful but deadly web of ice.

Agnoix had a death grip on the side of the mining pod, and willed herself not to think of the cold seeping into her mining suit. How her life depended on a tank of air less than a third full. She hoped it would be enough. She watched as her friend Cassidy pushed off, floating towards the portal between dimensions.

It's beautiful, Cassidy thought as she pushed off from the mining pod and got her first proper look of outer space. *Even with so many asteroids, the light from the stars pokes through. Thanks to the headlights of the mining pod, I can see the minerals with the rocks reflecting the light.* Cassidy only had a few moments to enjoy the starry view before the portal dominated the scene. *Gamgee was right, this portal is invisible, but its effects are noticeable.* Cassidy watched as the minute dust particles swirled around the edges of the round portal, caught forever on the lip of the doorway.

Agnoix was right about the dust... and Cassidy remembered the youthful Xik'en woman who saved her life. Almost to the portal, Cassidy tried to turn around to see her friend one last time, but found it difficult in Zero G, and despaired. A memory of her ponytail hitting her in the face gave her an idea. Reaching behind her, Cassidy grabbed the tail of her spacesuit and the Vao stones within it and threw it away from her. That slight motion was enough to cause Cassidy to spin, and just as her back touched the open portal she saw Agnoix standing in the open cockpit. As she waved goodbye to Agnoix, Cassidy slipped back through the portal.

CHAPTER SIXTEEN

The abrupt transition from the weightlessness of space to the gravity of Earth hit Cassidy like a punch in the gut. Even encased in the Xik'en spacesuit, Cassidy could still hear the roar of her body falling through the atmosphere. Instinct and training kicked in. Before Cassidy knew what she was doing, she twisted herself around so that she was falling face first and spread her arms and legs wide to increase her drag. The tail of the Xik'en spacesuit even helped keep her level.

Okay, where the heck am I? Cassidy thought as she fell to the blue ocean below.

Looking at her left wrist without turning her head, for fear of getting whiplash, Cassidy saw that her beacon was still flashing a bright red.

That's good. Gamgee didn't think radio signals could pass through portals, so that means the rescue boat must be nearby. Sharing a common frequency was a smart move.

Without an altimeter, Cassidy didn't know how high she was above the water, and had to rely on her experience and looking at the curvature of the horizon and the setting.

Seeing as her spacesuit still had a quarter tank, Cassidy decided that she would rather spend her time in the sky than treading water in the bulky suit. Cassidy yanked on her parachute's ripcord and prayed it still worked.

As the leader shot and the lines trailing with it unfurled, Cassidy crossed her fingers and hoped that all the rough and tumble adventures of the past day hadn't damaged the parachute.

I'll know soon enough, she thought as the parachute unfurled, filled full of air, and snapped her head back and forth. She hit her forehead against the alien helmet.

"That will leave a nasty bump," Cassidy said, and risked the higher elevation and the dangers of lower oxygen by opening the helmet.

As the smell of Earth's air filled Cassidy's lungs, she smiled until her face hurt. She made long winding spirals through the sky to hunt for the rescue boat, using the beacon as a guide.

Good, clean air... I don't know how much longer I could have lasted in that muggy soup the Xik'ens called air without sprouting mushrooms.

Thinking of Xik'en and her experience there, Cassidy reflected on how the outcome would have been disastrous without Agnoix.

I hope her fellow people aren't too hard on her; I know she pretended it would all be okay to put my fears at ease, but I can't help feeling like I abandoned her. It sounds like only her father supports her freethinking ideas. He's rarely around and she has to deal with that brother of hers and a mother trying to make her conform to proper Xik'en society.

It's not all that different with me and my sisters. Ditch-

ing me to hang with their friends, teasing me for loving history books rather than those silly TV shows. Is what I did to Agnoix any different from what my sisters did to me?

With this thought rattling around in her mind, Cassidy vowed to contact her sisters when she got home and reforge their relationships.

With her mind settled, Cassidy noticed that her wrist beacon was flashing steadily. She saw the glint of the rescue boat as the setting sun reflected off its hull.

Using the D rings to steer her parachute towards the craft, her heart skipped a beat when she saw a flare reach skyward, signaling that they had seen her.

As Cassidy skimmed around the waves mere meters below, she closed the helmet on the spacesuit to keep the water out and splashed into the Atlantic Ocean.

She bobbed like a cork, even with her tail and its five pounds of rocks within it hanging below her. Cassidy floated on her back after the tricky task of releasing the chute with gloves made for Xik'en hands.

As the rescue boat came up beside her, its wake making her rise and fall like a message in a bottle, Cassidy opened her visor and shouted to the crew leaning over the railing ready to grab her.

"Hurry, would you guys? It's been a heck of a day and I'm starved. Does anyone have a sandwich handy?"

CHAPTER SEVENTEEN

"Easy there Agnoix, hold it together for a few minutes more," Agnoix said to herself as she guided the mining pod, with the remains of Cassidy's plane still in its grip, into the mining bay they had fled hours before.

She knew she shouldn't have done it. She should have closed the hatch of the mining pod as soon as Cassidy had exited the tiny craft. But Agnoix did not want to miss seeing her friend transition through the portal. There was no flash or anything: Cassidy just flowed through the portal, her waving hand the last thing to pass through into another dimension.

With cramped muscles that never warmed up after being exposed to the cold of space, Agnoix had started the trip back to her home on the mining station. It hadn't been as easy as Agnoix had led Cassidy to believe, but after some trial and error she figured out the instruments and activated the locator scanner. All Agnoix had had to do then was follow the path on the screen to exit the asteroid field, right into a swarm of mining pods and security barges, their powerful lasers aimed at her.

Agnoix's frantic and confused rambling over the radio had been enough to convince everyone that the "murderous mammal" was no longer on board.

Her 'escort' and its weapons watched as she flew into the mining bay, Cassidy's plane still gripped tight.

While no longer the madhouse it had been when she and Cassidy had left the mining bay, there were emergency crews putting out small fires and making equipment safe. When the work crews had fled the bay, they left a trail of jammed and overloaded equipment in their wake.

"Someone must have made some calls," Agnoix whispered in dread as she saw that her mother, Axaik, a dozen security personal, and hundreds of workers awaited her.

Not that anyone was noticing her landing, but without a bump, Agnoix landed the pod and lowered Cassidy's plane to the floor.

"I wonder if it's too late to follow Cassidy," Agnoix mumbled as she popped the cockpit hatch and tried not to struggle as two members of the security service marched her towards her fate.

Scale rot. Mom looks really mad, I wonder how much of the truth she knows? She looked at her brother, who appeared under the weather. *At least it appears Axaik is paying for his indulgence with the Grove juice -- serves him right.*

Orlol snapped at her daughter, cutting off Agnoix's thoughts. "Are you all right?"

Head hanging in shame and tail flicking, Agnoix replied: "Yes mother, I'm not hurt," and then almost fell over as she was enveloped into a massive hug, the first in recent memory from her mother.

"I was so worried when they told me that this mammal kidnapped you and made you its hostage. It did nothing 'unnatural' to you, did it dear?" Orlol asked, and started patting down her daughter as if to check for bite marks.

"I'm fine Mom, Cas... the Creature, the warm-blood didn't hurt me, it just scared me."

An elderly Xik'en walked up, ending the mother-daughter moment by slapping his tail against the floor for attention.

"Young one, my name is Xizik and I'm senior administrator for this mining station. I need you to tell me what happened. Take your time, tell me everything."

And with her mother's taloned hand on her shoulder for support, Agnoix told the story that she and Cassidy had came up with, with a few addictions.

Agnoix told of how she rescued 'the mammal' not knowing what it was, only knowing that it was someone in danger and that she had done what any dutiful Xik'en citizen would do, which garnered her a nod from the senior administrator. She threw her brother a bone and covered her own tail, saying that Axaik had tried to save his younger sister from the warm-blood and that he had suffered an injury in the attempt. Any poor behaviour since then was likely because of the injury and the shock of not being able to rescue his sister.

I hope you realize what I'm doing for you, brother. I just saved your scales, so you keep your mouth shut about how friendly Cassidy and I were.

There was a surprised look on Axaik's face, which turned to puzzlement when Senior Administrator Xizik turned to him.

"Is this true young man?"

Axaik's puzzlement dawned into understanding, then he nodded. "Yes, yes, like she said. I tried to save her."

"My children are good Xik'en citizens, Senior Administrator. My husband and I raised them right." Orlol stood proudly and squeezed Agnoix's shoulder.

"Hmmm... yes, I see. Continue child."

Agnoix finished her tale as planned.

"And after that, Sir, I travelled back to the mining station with the alien's vessel in tow," Agnoix said to divert the conversation, and walked towards Cassidy's plane.

"Yes, yes. Splendid job, ah... Agnoix," Xizik said as he walked up to the plane. "Our scientists will have to study this craft, but to my untrained eye it looks rather primitive. These mammals care little for their lives or the lives of others. But I must prepare us for any future incursions..."

"I agree, Senior Administrator, and it's an excellent idea," Agnoix said, hijacking the politicians speech. "We must be vigilant and strong, and to do that we must know our enemy. We can no longer hide behind our walls and wait for the worlds to come to us. We must go out and seek them and study them for our own defense and the security of the great Xik'en Interstellar Empire," Agnoix finished in a shout.

I think I might have spent too much time with Cassidy; I didn't know I had that in me.

For the space of a couple heartbeats, the whole mining bay was quiet. Everyone stared at the young Xik'en woman, perplexed and confused by the unexpected speech, when Axaik thumped his tail against the floor in approval.

Orlol followed suit, then more and more of the onlookers.

Seizing the moment, Agnoix walked beside Senior Administrator Xizik, gripped his talons in hers, and raised them both to the sky, and the applause of Xik'en tails was thunderous.

EPILOGUE

Xizik stepped into the shadowed dark of the solitary confinement wing of the Xik'en penitentiary. It was a narrow room with cells on either side and floors covered with sawdust, with a single light hanging from overhead casting strange, oblong shadows on the walls all around.

"We had an interesting event today, Tallis," he said, stopping at a hand washing station in the center of the hall and scrubbing. He picked up a portable light from a dispensary beneath the station and flicked it on, its bright rectangle shimmering out into the void. He stepped past each cell, shining the light into each in turn along the way and examining the sorrow-filled faces within. "Had a visitor top side. Caused a lot of trouble... almost as much as you did."

He continued from one sad face to the next, finally landing on one that was not full of fear or anguish. Its lip was curled up into a rueful sneer. It was also human. He glared back out at Xizik, sitting at the far wall of his cage with his legs tucked up around him.

"I'd like you to tell me if you know anything about that, Tallis."

Tallis turned, running a finger along the dozens of tally marks that ran the length of his cell's stone wall, feeling the gouges of them absently. Despite his circumstance, he looked bored. There was a small, thin stress ball in his other hand that he rolled liberally between his fingers. "Why would I know anything about anything that happened outside these walls, Xizik?" he said, his voice somewhere in the realm between bemused and contemptuous.

"Because, Tallis. She was human."

Tallis turned and glared at Xizik, a light behind his eyes that had not been there in months. Even though he tried to hide it, he started to smile.

ACKNOWLEDGEMENTS

The authors would like to pay special thanks to the *Slipstreamers* committee at Engen Books, including Amanda Labonté, Matthew LeDrew, AJ Ryan, Ellen Curtis, Erin Vance, and, Lauralana Dunne.

Without their tireless efforts, none of this would have been possible.

Special thanks to this episode's editor, Ali House.

COMING SOON!
THE LOTUS FOUNTAIN
BY JD RYOT & NICOLE LITTLE!

The next incredible episode of Slipstreamers, The Lotus Fountain, will be available soon, written with Nicole Little!

While trying to live her best normal life, Cassidy discovers a secret portal to stunning world of Lotus Lorea, a world populated only by women! At first things seem ideallic... but not everything is as it seems, and the waters of the Lotus Fountain may hide the secrets to immortal life!

SPECIAL BONUS STORIES!

We're pleased to present eight additional stories from this episode's co-author, Peter J Foote. Presented here are *Sea Monkies, Bubble Babe, Burning Bridges, Forced Migration, Guest Rights, Invisible Neighbour, Little Star and the Shepherdess, Kids These Days...*

Peter J Foote is one of only three authors as of this publication to be included in all of the *From the Rock* series short story collections, and is recognized as a gifted crafter of short fiction.

From the Rock is a series of anthologies from Engen Books exploring young adult takes on a variety of genres from authors around Atlantic Canada.

SEA MONKIES

Tiny fingers dig into beach sand until foaming sea water fills the hole. Shelby unfolds the envelope she found in the old comic book and sprinkles dried eggs which disappear into seawater.

"Please work," Shelby says biting her lip.

Peeling apart the envelope, Shelby folds the waxed paper into a lopsided boat. Digging hands into pockets, she places seven jelly beans inside the bobbing craft, the setting sun reflecting off the water.

The morning sun chases Shelby down the beach, her flip-flops slapping the wet sand.

Peering into the pool, Shelby finds a mermaid smaller than her pinkie finger lounging inside the paper boat, iridescent tail hanging over the side. The mermaid cradles a purple jelly bean covered in tiny bite marks, looks up at Shelby and smiles, jelly bean smeared on her face.

"The purple ones are my favourite too," Shelby says, her grin turning into a sad frown. "I can't stay, school starts tomorrow."

Ears drooping, the mermaid balances the jelly bean one-handed and points to the open water.

"You have to go home too?"

With a sad smile, the mermaid nods, tail swirling in the water, scales sparkling.

Kneeling in the wet sand, Shelby digs a channel allowing the incoming tide to connect with the pool. The gentle ocean waves grab the paper boat as it bobs through the breach, her jelly beans around her, the smiling mermaid waves goodbye.

"It was nice meeting you, I hope we met again!" Shelby calls out.

BUBBLE BABE

Timothy peeks out his bedroom window and watches his mother climb into Nathan's SUV.

"About frigging time!" Timothy says with delight and dashes to his school backpack. Trembling hands reveal a padded envelope, covered in Chinese lettering.

Cradling it, Timothy dashes to the bathroom and locks the door before tearing open the envelope. Inside is a clear bottle, filled with thick ribbons of pink and cream coloured liquid, labelled "Bubble babe."

Jamming the plug into the bathtub drain, Timothy turns on the hot water. Breaking the seal on the bottle he gets a whiff of the liquid, strawberries, clean hair, and air after a storm. With a deep sigh Timothy pours the thick liquid into the steaming hot water. He makes long gentle strokes as the translated instructions listed.

Wringing his hands together Timothy waits for something to happen and soon the pink and cream liquid twirls within the hot water and bubbles form.

Instead of popping when they reach the surface, they lay on top. They connect to each other and in minutes the rough form of a female body lays in the tub.

"Is that it?" says Timothy in a disappointed tone.

Perhaps in answer, the bubbles move around each other. They split and divide faster and faster until there is a beautiful naked woman laying in the foam-filled tub. She takes a deep breath causing Timothy to jump, and her eyes open and find his. "Hi Handsome" she says.

BURNING BRIDGES

"I must destroy this prison if I'm ever to be free of its grip." Whispers Missy as she leaps from the dollhouse to the table.

Missy listens for any change in the giants snoring before sneaking through the maze of empty beer bottles to the open box of matches. She struggles to remove one of the massive wooden sticks, her arms trembling.

With a thrust against the side of the box, the match flares to life, startling Missy and making her bump into a bottle causing it to "clinks" with its neighbour.

"What's happening?" the giant asks, his voice thick with sleep.

Missy leaps back into the dollhouse dragging the lit match behind her lighting curtains and tablecloths in her wake. The dollhouse shakes as the giant grips it, Missy stumbles across the living room, the match threatening to light her gown or singe her hair.

Picking herself up, she sees the giant peering into the dollhouse. The flames consuming the dollhouse highlight the broken nose and beady eyes of the creature.

"This cursed dwelling will never again trap one of

my kind!" Missy yells into the face of the giant. The face retreats and a gigantic hand reaches through the flames, hunting for her.

With a surge of speed, Missy dashes through flames and charges out the front door of the dollhouse and back into her own realm. The flaming portal between worlds slammed shut behind her, Missy collapses in the snow, home at last.

FORCED MIGRATION

"Craftsmen assemble!" the Queen of the ants commands.

The drones lower their thorax in respect. "We went forth as directed, North, South, East, and West and all detected the invisible barrier, there's no sign of our homeland or a way out of this realm."

"And the..." the queen's antennae wiggle skyward.

Bowing deeper, one drone responds. "The Goddess... she's always looking down on us my queen, she's everywhere, the whole world is under her gaze. My Queen, why is she a..."

With a snap of her pinchers, the Queen cuts off further chatter from her drones. "Go back to your labours. The Goddess has given us this new land, so we must make it our own and build a new colony in her glory. Be gone!"

As the ant craftsmen scurry from their audience with their queen, one drone whispers to its companions, "Why do you suppose the Queen cut me off?"

Shaking their antennae, another replies, "Foolish ant, the Queen can't acknowledge that the Goddess is a... you know."

"A mammal?"

"Quiet you fool, if she hears you we're done for, everyone knows the Goddess is an insect. Let's go back to our labours and leave the nature of divinity to others."

***

"Mama?"

"Yes, Danielle?"

"Do you think the ants are happy in their new home? They're running around the glass walls like they're confused or scared."

"I'm sure they'll settle down soon dear, now get your face out of that jar and wash your hands for supper."

GUEST RIGHTS

"What's all that racket outside steward? I'm eating my second supper." Roars King Latchbreaker of the Gnomes around a mouthful of roasted squirrel.

The steward bows before his portly monarch. "A member of the Elven Court who is on her way to the Fairy Queen and has become delayed by the weather and claims Guest Rights my liege."

"Stuffy elves, never there when needed, and around when not wanted, send her away!" A drumstick thrust for emphasis.

"My King!" the steward cries, "Our alliance with the Elves! Guest Rights."

"Yes, yes. A roof overhead, a meal, and safe passage. I remember." King Latchbreaker mumbles. Surveying his throne room with its earthen floor and ceiling of intertwined roots the king shakes his head. "She won't fit down here, find her a place in the stables with the battle toads."

The stewards lip twists but he gives a tiny nod. "And a meal?"

"Elves being so refined wouldn't like our rustic fare,

I'm sure the larder has nuts and berries."

"I will see to something appropriate my liege." the steward rises but King Latchbreaker hasn't finished.

"As for safe passage through our kingdom for such an important guest, I think it's only right YOU escort her."

"But... but my liege, that journey will take days."

"I know, now attend to our guest steward." As King Latchbreaker watches his steward shuffle out of the throne room he says, "Serves you right for disturbing my second supper!"

INVISIBLE NEIGHBOUR

Tavaril walks through the forest, fresh snow muffles her footsteps, the afternoon's sunlight throws shadows through naked branches, she could almost believe she was alone.

But she knows she's not, her invisible friend is close.

Proof when her favourite satin ribbon, lost in a windstorm a week ago flutters from a tree. Smiling, Tavaril uncoils it from the branch and ties her hair, the ribbon back where it belongs.

"Thank you" she whispers into the empty forest and continues her stroll.

Her destination in sight, Tavaril stops at the foot of the crumbling keep and discovers the stone steps brushed free of snow, her lips curve in a smile.

Her cloak billowing behind her as she rushes to the top of the stairs, Tavaril smells the steeped herbal tea and fresh bread before she sees the picnic basket set up on the fallen column. No other soul in sight.

Lifting the cloth covering the basket, Tavaril spies her favourite, nut bread still warm from the oven.

"You better be careful, the baker knows someone is

stealing his wares, we can't have an innocent taking the blame. I'll make sure it gets paid for, now why don't you come out and join me?"

As Tavaril pours the tea and slices thick portions of bread, she notes a darkened corner of the ruin take shapes as vines pull away from stone walls. Her invisible friend, cloaked in a mantle of ivy, joins her for a picnic.

KIDS THESE DAYS...

"Whoa there young Miss. This is a private party, do you have the password?" the toad guarding the door says to the young elf trying to sneak into the tavern.

"Password..." the elven girl stammers, her wide eyes reflecting the lights escaping around the door. "Please sir, can I enter? The Pixie Chicks are my favourite band and when I heard they were playing at this tavern, I knew I had to come."

His throat puffed out, the toad replies. "Tell you what young lady, you answer my riddle and I'll let you sneak in, agreed?"

The rising chorus of the band and the roar of the crowd aren't loud enough to wash away the young elves reply. "Yes! I must see them, they understand life and true love like no one else..." She stops in a panic as the toad turns away. "No wait! Ask your riddle please!"

His face serious, the toad clears his throat and recites; "What never asks questions, but is always answered. What am I?"

Her eyes squint and she repeats the riddle to herself, the crowd inside crying out for another song, and then a bright beaming smile crosses the elven girl's face as she exclaims; "A door".

With a wink and a nod, the toad hops aside and allows the young elf to rush into the loud tavern, her face alight in joy. The toad chuckles to himself, "Kids these days..."

LITTLE STAR AND THE SHEPHERDESS

"Hello little star, are you awake?" Emma whispers through the panels of the door to the mud brick lamb pen where she had rolled the wounded star several days ago.

The soft golden light inside beats a steady rhythm as a response, provoking a smile to cross Emma's face. Crouching beside the door, Emma thinks back to how she had discovered the injured star while searching for a wayward lamb.

Blackened and battered, the tiny star had plummeted to earth after being knocked out of the heavens. Her heart filled with compassion, Emma rolled the flickering star into the safety of the lamb pen before the rising sun could weaken it further.

Every night since, Emma rolls out the weak star so it can bathe in the light of its brethren. Opening the rough door, Emma reaches into the pen and rolls out the tiny star running her fingers over the polished surface.

"Whole again, and your light is steady, I believe you will be strong enough to fly tonight," Emma says in a soft voice as she caresses the golden orb.

With the star in her lap, Emma raises her face to the

heavens and sings. As the wordless song builds to a climax, she raises the star with both hands and releases it. The tiny star fades for a second before bursting in intensity and streaks skyward.

With a smile and a tear in her eye, the shepherdess watches her tiny star until daybreak.

ON SALE NOW FROM ENGEN BOOKS

When fifteen-year-old Phoenix loses her caregiver, everyone that she has ever known inexplicably turn their backs on her. Given the impossible burden of repaying an unknown debt, Phoenix sets out on her own with her trusty donkey, Muler, as her only companion.A chance encounter with Malcourt, a mysterious traveller, not only saves her life, but sets it on a trajectory that she would have never thought possible.

ABOUT THE AUTHOR

Peter J. Foote is a bestselling speculative fiction writer from Nova Scotia, Canada. He runs the FictionFirst Used Books, specializing in fantasy & sci-fi titles. Peter's stories are a reflection of his personal life, as he is a firm believer in the adage that a writer should write what they know.

Peter's work has twice been awarded the Kit Sora Flash Fiction Prize and holds the distinction of being one the only authors to be featured in all the From the Rock collections. In total, Peter has been featured in over two dozen publications, with interest in his short fiction worldwide.

He is the founder of the Genre Writers of Atlantic Canada group.

JD Ryot is the reclusive creator of the *Slipstreamers* series from Engen Books. JD is an avid fan of young adult literature and adventure serials. When asked if they had come to this world through a portal themselves, JD Ryot refused to answer. No record of their birth has ever been found... on this world.